"OPEN UP," LUKE INSTRUCTED.

Cassie popped her mouth open in a wide and exaggerated pose. He grasped her chin between his fingers to inspect her throat. Their eyes met briefly.

"It's just a himple caze of tonsihites," she garbled as he held her mouth firmly open.

"Could be," he murmured distractedly. "But then tonciletiemosis has the same symptoms."

She frowned. "Whut's 'at?"

"A rare, debilitating disease that . . . oh surely you've heard of it."

"I'b neber heard ob suzh a diseese!" she scoffed, but her pulse did give a queer little leap at the mere thought of such a malady.

"You're serious? Well," he said in a grim tone, "the voice goes first, then the eyes . . . then the mouth . . . well, let's just say it's a heck of a way to go."

CANDLELIGHT ECSTASY CLASSIC ROMANCES

CANDLELIGHT ECSTASY ROMANCES®

TUG OF WAR

Lori Copeland

A CANDLELIGHT ECSTASY ROMANCE®

Published by
Dell Publishing Co., Inc.
1 Dag Hammarskjold Plaza
New York, New York 10017

Dell ® TM 681510, Dell Publishing Co., Inc.

Candlelight Ecstasy Romance®, 1,203,540, is a registered
trademark of Dell Publishing Co., Inc., New York, New York.

ISBN: 0-440-19021-5

Printed in the United States of America

December 1986

10 9 8 7 6 5 4 3 2 1

WFH

To Our Readers:

We have been delighted with your enthusiastic response to Candlelight Ecstasy Romances®, and we thank you for the interest you have shown in this exciting series.

In the upcoming months we will continue to present the distinctive sensuous love stories you have come to expect only from Ecstasy. We look forward to bringing you many more books from your favorite authors and also the very finest work from new authors of contemporary romantic fiction.

As always, we are striving to present the unique, absorbing love stories that you enjoy most—books that are more than ordinary romance. Your suggestions and comments are always welcome. Please write to us at the address below.

Sincerely,

The Editors
Candlelight Romances
1 Dag Hammarskjold Plaza
New York, New York 10017

TUG OF WAR

CHAPTER ONE

To just say that it was a beautiful day would be doing an injustice to Mother Nature.

The sky was that brilliant, breathtaking blue that makes a person want to lie out under a big old shade tree and stare at its magnificence for hours on end. A soft breeze teased the air with the tantalizing smell of the flowers blooming colorfully along the highway, and Cass rolled down the car windows to allow the achingly familiar smells of her childhood to recapture her senses.

The verdant, gentle swells of the hillsides spread out before her with open arms, as if to say they welcomed one of their children home once again.

She took a deep, intoxicating breath of the sweet air and let it out slowly. New York City was wonderful, full of excitement and a million new things to see and do every day, but Rueter Flats, Texas, was home and always would be.

Actually, she was just a little surprised to find that she was looking forward to coming home for her vacation this year.

Always before there had been a tiny seed of resentment nagging at her when she would have to spend her precious few weeks of freedom in Rueter Flats, but somehow this year seemed different.

With a touch of renewed guilt, she was reminded of the fact that she hadn't seen her parents in well over two years and it was no wonder that they were beginning to get annoyed with her continuing excuses.

And to be honest she had seriously toyed with the idea of giving them yet another reason as to why she wouldn't be home again this summer, but then she reminded herself that they were getting along in years and she wouldn't always have them around to make excuses to.

Oh, they had all been perfectly valid excuses. There had been that bad snowstorm last Christmas and she had decided to stay in the city for the holidays instead of making the long trip home. And the year before that she had decided to take advantage of an unexpected Aspen ski trip instead of taking a summer vacation.

But this year it was time to stop making excuses and pay an obligatory visit home.

Maybe it wouldn't be so bad this time. The weather certainly looked as if it would cooperate and she had to admit the slow, lackadaisical way of life of the citizens of Rueter Flats would be a far cry from the hustle and bustle of New York.

So absorbed in her thoughts, she nearly whizzed by her intended cutoff. She slammed on her brakes, came to a dead halt for a moment, then hurriedly backed up to make the turn, chuckling softly under her breath at the thought of what a pileup that would have brought on in the city.

Concentrate on your driving, Cass, she reminded

10

herself as she shifted her sleek silver Jaguar into second gear and gunned it on down the road.

Once again her thoughts drifted back to years past as she sped along the back roads leading to her childhood home.

She was quite sure that leaving Rueter Flats wasn't on the high-priority list of most women of that town, but it had always been high on hers.

Oh, it was a nice town. She couldn't argue that. It was just small and exceedingly dull with a population of around fifteen hundred. But by now Ellie Sweetwood would surely have done her best to increase that statistic. She shook her head with amusement at the thought of her former childhood friend and schoolmate. When Ellie Poston married Teft Sweetwood she became a baby machine, but then there were a lot of women in Rueter Flats who were like that.

Now, take her sisters for instance. They were having kids with alarming regularity and they couldn't be happier. They would smile and simply shrug their shoulders when an impending birth was announced and state without apology that they were married to their "good ole boys," whom they laughingly said kept them "barefoot and pregnant" most of the time.

Their husbands were barely eking out a decent living on their small scraps of land, but not one of them ever raised a voice in complaint.

But they couldn't help but be thrilled with Cass's new life. She had such an exciting, glamorous life, while they on the other hand had the same boring, monotonous existence day after day.

Clearly they thought the sun rose and set in their

"successful" sister, yet, strangely enough, never once had any one of them expressed a desire to trade places with her.

Their eyes may have shone with pride when Cass came home and regaled them with stories of the advertising world, but that light was decidedly pale compared to the one that glowed so radiantly when they looked at their husbands or cradled one of their sleepy children's heads against their bosoms after a long day of picnicking and swimming with all the McCason family gathered about them.

Cass had never been able to understand their complete contentment. Their way of life was a far cry from what she wanted. Being a dirt farmer and raising a passel of towheaded kids wasn't for her, and once more a tremendous feeling of gratitude washed over her when she thought about what her parents had sacrificed in order to scrape up enough money to put her through college.

But it had paid off, and the right person had an opportunity to view her work, and before she knew it she had landed a job with one of the most prestigious advertising agencies on Madison Avenue.

Now their daughter was settled in a career that afforded her luxuries that her parents had only heard about. Cass had been bright, talented, and eager to achieve, and each year brought her one more step up the ladder of success. Yes, for a girl who came from practically nothing but a hole in the road in Texas, who was now driving a Jaguar, living in a luxury apartment in the heart of Manhattan plus enjoying a career that was going nowhere but up—well, she wasn't doing bad at all.

She heaved a sigh of pure contentment. Yes, sir. The rest of the McCasons could have her share of the farm life. She'd take the big city any day.

A swell of pride engulfed her as she thought about the newest piece of information she had to pass on. What would her family think when they heard of this latest advancement at work? In September, when Rolland Hendricks retired, Cassandra Beth McCason was going to be made vice president of Creble and Associates. Sure, there was more than one vice president at Creble's, but still the title was impressive.

Mom and Pop would be proud when they heard that bit of news. They would probably throw one of those big parties they were forever having and invite the entire town to come and celebrate their daughter's newest success. Her relatives would gather from miles around to see the little McCason gal who had gone to the big city and struck it rich. She had to snicker at that thought. She was a far cry from rich, but she had to admit she was doing extremely well. And it felt good.

No longer did she have to shop at the local discount stores for her clothes and save up for weeks just to purchase some small luxury item she wanted. She was wearing cashmere and pearls now. And having her hair styled in the finest salons instead of having to wash it herself, and eating croissants for breakfast every morning instead of corn flakes.

Now if she wanted anything, she just whipped out her American Express Card and bought it.

A small smile of satisfaction tugged at the corners of her mouth as she sped along. In fact, she was at the point now where she was buying things she really didn't need simply because it felt good.

Yes, sir. No more grubbing in the dirt for Cass McCason.

She had it made.

About eight dogs of assorted breeds ran out to meet her as her car turned across the old cattle guard, their yelps setting up enough racket to wake the dead. Nipping at the shiny chrome rims of the fancy sports car, they chased it down the rutted lane until she brought the car to a halt in front of a weather-beaten, two-story farmhouse that seemed forever in need of a new coat of paint.

At the sound of all the clamor the front door flew open and two happy children clamored off the porch and headed for Cass as fast as their little legs could carry them. She cringed as she saw the condition of their hands as they whooped around the car like a bunch of wild Indians and somehow managed to touch every square inch of the shiny new vehicle before she could bring it to a complete halt.

"Oh, boy! Auntie Cass. This here's a neat car," the older of the two proclaimed in awe. "I bet it costed lots of money, huh?" His chubby hands ran reverently down the length of the car as he circled it excitedly.

Cass hurriedly got out of the car and slammed the door shut. She raced around the side of the car and put out a beseeching hand. "Yes, lots of money. Please, Billy Ray, don't touch the hood that way!"

"Gosh, is it neato," the smaller one chimed in as three of the bigger dogs, still yapping at the tops of their lungs, jumped up on Cass and started to lap at her face.

Staggering under the weight of the smelly animals, she felt her Gucci heel sink down in the soft ground at the precise moment her eyes took note of one of the speckled bird dogs doing his "thing" on the rim of her tire.

"Billy Ray! Get that dog!" she demanded.

Billy Ray was too busy inspecting the fascinating new object that had just pulled into his drive to heed Cass's frantic pleas.

"I'll get him, Auntie Cath," the smaller boy offered, and before she could stop him he had picked up a large rock and hurled it in the direction of the dog, who was still standing next to the car.

"No! Bobby Ray!" But her words came too late.

The sickening thud of the rock striking the car caused Cass to shut her eyes in despair and sag against the car weakly as the remainder of the dogs gathered around her feet, still barking rambunctiously.

"There, Auntie Cath. He'th going now." The child grinned proudly as the bird dog quickly lost interest in the new company and sauntered away from the car in search of a shade tree.

"What in the world is going on out here?" The screen door swung open and a plump, silver-haired woman stepped out on the porch and shaded her eyes to see what all the commotion was about.

Her eyes lit with joy when Neoma McCason saw her youngest daughter slumped against the car, smiling weakly back at her.

"Hi, Mom."

"Cassie!" With amazing agility for a woman her

15

age, Neoma was off the porch and hurrying toward the car as Cass jerked her shoe out of the dirt and inspected the grubby heel that was caked with mud.

By now her mother had reached the car and engulfed her in a big bear hug as she laughed and returned the embrace eagerly.

"Hi, Mom."

"Hi, darlin'. I wasn't expectin' you until late this evening." For a moment Cass closed her eyes and drank in the familiar smell that held her tightly pressed against an ample bosom. Neoma always smelled like freshly laundered clothes and homemade bread, with just the tiniest scent of roses mixed in.

"I made better time than I thought I would," Cass told her as she wrapped her arm around her mom's waist and they began walking toward the house. "Where's Pop?"

"Down in the barn. He's got a sick calf he's been working with all day." Neoma looked her daughter over hungrily, her generous mouth breaking into another huge smile. "My, you look good, honey. Real good. And that fancy new car! Is that yours?"

"Yeah." Cass grinned back. "Pretty nice, huh?"

"Never seen anything like it," Neoma marveled, her gaze running pridefully over the shiny sports car.

"It's a Jaguar," Cass announced proudly, just as if that would ring any bell with her mother. To Neoma a Jaguar was an animal. Always had been and always would be.

"Oh? Well, it's right nice," she praised, then diverted her attention to the two rowdy boys still racing around the fancy automobile. "Billy Ray and Bobby Ray, you git on down to the barn with your grandpa.

16

We don't want you puttin' any scratches up your Aunt Cass's new car."

Too late for that, Cass thought as her eyes grimly searched for further signs of missing paint on the fender where Bobby Ray had thrown the rock.

"Aw, Grandma!" They both raised their voices in protest as Neoma shot them a warning look. "No back talkin', now. You go on and do what I say before I take a switch to your behinds!"

The boys grumbled a few more chosen words between them before they raced off to seek other pursuits.

"They're really growing," Cass marveled as they walked toward the house.

"Like ragweed," Neoma sighed. "The baby's in the house. You've never seen Joey Ray, have you?"

"No, just pictures of him." It never ceased to amaze her the way her sister had named all her children after their father. You would think one Ray in the family would have been enough, but no, in addition to the father being named Ray, there was Billy Ray, Bobby Ray, and now Joey Ray.

"How is Rosalee?" Cass inquired of her middle sister.

"Why, she's as healthy as a horse. She left the kids with me today. Had a doctor's appointment." Neoma grinned knowingly. "She thinks she might be in the family way again."

Cass shook her head in amazement. "Lord, I hope not."

"Why, Cass McCason. What a thing to say," her mother admonished, clearly shocked that her daughter

17

would say such a thing. "Her and Ray want another baby."

"Why in the world would she want another child? They have three already, and the baby's not even a year old yet. How many more Rays can the family stand?"

"Ray says he wants a whole house full before he stops," Neoma laughed.

"Well, he's certainly on his way," Cass acknowledged as they stepped up on the porch.

"I'll have to call Rowena and Rachel and Pauly and Newt to let them know you're in early. They're all a-comin' over for supper, but they'll want to come sooner when they find out you're home," Neoma was saying.

A tiny shudder ran through Cass as she thought about her brother and sisters and all their families under one roof, but she tried to force as much enthusiasm into her voice as she could. It wasn't that she didn't love every one of them, it was just when they all got together everything was so . . . disorganized and boisterous. "Yes . . . I'll be glad to see all of them again. . . ."

Both women glanced up as a late-model pickup came rolling into the yard and the driver gave a couple of toots on the horn in a friendly fashion and stuck his arm out the window to wave at Neoma.

Neoma smiled and waved at the driver as he proceeded on down to the barn lot.

"Who was that?"

"That's the Travers boy—Luke, you remember him, don't you?"

"Oh, brother. That wild hair." Cass remembered

18

him all right. He had been a thorn in her side the entire time they had been growing up.

He had pestered her unmercifully in grade school, terrorized her in junior high, and by the time they had reached high school she had stopped speaking to him altogether.

That had never seemed to bother him, though. In fact, it had become a little game between them to turn their noses up at each other every chance they got, and living in such a small town, that was quite often.

But along about the time they both graduated she had dismissed Luke Travers from her mind, and last she had heard he had left town to join the Navy, which was probably the best thing that could ever have happened to Rueter Flats.

Her gaze absently followed the pickup until it stopped in front of the barn.

But apparently the bad seed had returned.

As wild as Luke Travers had been, Cass wouldn't have been a bit surprised to hear he was off making license plates in the big house somewhere.

Neoma chuckled at Cass's disgruntled observation of Luke. "Yes, he used to be quite a rounder in his younger days, but the boy's really settled down since he came home. Dad and I were talking about just how much he's changed the other night."

"Boy? Really, Mom. He's hardly a boy any longer. He's my age or older," Cass reminded.

"Well, thirty years old isn't exactly ancient," Neoma agreed good-naturedly as she opened the screen door to the kitchen. "Luke's turned out to be a real fine man, Cass. He's the local vet around here and your little brother Wylie's taken a real likin' to him."

19

"A veterinarian! Luke Travers is a veterinarian!" Now that was hard to swallow. He had barely made passing grades in high school because he was too busy getting into trouble all the time.

At the mention of her youngest brother Cass's face clouded with concern. "You mean you actually let Wylie associate with him? Now what in the world would a nine-year-old have in common with a thirty-year-old, Mom? Especially that thirty-year-old!"

"Now why should that upset you?" A slow grin spread across her features again. "Oh, my. I had forgotten. You and Luke never did get along, did you?"

"No, we didn't. I didn't like him and he didn't like me."

Neoma clucked in a motherly fashion. "Never could understand why. I have to admit he was a might ornery at times, but I don't think he was all that bad."

"Oh no? Then how come every time anything bad happened in this town they went looking for Luke Travers?"

" 'Cause he usually was the one who did it," Neoma had to agree. "Either him or that Falk boy, but that was a long time ago, honey, and they were usually just harmless little pranks. When Luke came home from the service he had turned into a real fine man. Then he up and went off to college and before we knew it he was back with a handful of them real fancy-soundin' degrees," she boasted. "It turned out he had become a veterinarian and the people of the town welcomed him with open arms. You know the closest vet around Rueter Flats is old Milt Turner over in Macon and he's gettin' blind as a bat."

Cass could hardly believe Luke could be that

changed. Not the Luke who used to push over out-houses with people still sitting in them or throw sacks of burning cow manure on her front porch.

"I still find it hard to believe you would let Wylie associate with him," Cass complained.

"I don't see why not. They fish and hunt together all the time. Uriah's health isn't what it used to be, so Luke's been filling in for him. I appreciate the time he finds to spend with the boy."

"What's the matter with Pauly? Why can't he take Wylie hunting and fishing?" The thought of her little brother being in the company of someone as unsavory as Luke Travers annoyed her, especially when there were certainly enough men in the McCason family to provide that service quite sufficiently.

"He does when they have the chance, but Newt and Pauly have been real busy lately," Neoma excused. "And they have their own family to look after."

"Well, I don't like it," Cass complained once more as they walked into the large, airy kitchen.

The tantalizing smell of pot roast simmering in the oven filled the air as Cass paused and drank in the familiar surroundings.

This room—this house—had always been the same for as long as Cass could remember. It was as if she had walked out the door only twenty minutes ago instead of two years.

A massive round oak table sat in the middle of the room laden with jars of homemade jellies, pickles, and preserves her mother had set out for the evening meal.

She could see several delectably browned pies cooling on the counter and the smell of apples and cinnamon still mingled enticingly in the air with that of the pot roast.

The pictures Cass and her brothers and sisters had made in grade school hung on the brightly papered wall above the old refrigerator. Colorful rainbows and comical-looking stick characters that had the names Mom and Dad and Pauly and Cassie and Rachel and so on scrawled boldly beside them.

Newt had even attempted at the age of three to draw a picture of their old dog, Whiskers, and the family still went into hysterics at the finished product. The dog resembled a deranged chicken more than the valued family pet, but Newt still insisted there was a definite resemblance, so the picture had remained on display.

On the long oak buffet that sat along the wall were pictures of Grandma and Grandpa McCason and Grandpa and Grandma Kinley, plus a photograph of every child and grandchild of Neoma and Uriah.

There was one of Cassie in her prom dress and Newt in his high school cap and gown. There was Rachel and Jesse's wedding picture and Rosalee and Ray holding their first child and happily smiling into the camera. A beaming Cassie proudly displaying her college diploma and grinning, and Wylie wrestling on the front lawn with one of the dogs.

Crisply starched calico curtains hung at the glistening windows and the old linoleum was scrubbed to shiny perfection. Neoma McCason was well known for keeping a clean house, even though for years she had seven young children running in and out all day long.

Now there was only nine-year-old Wylie left at

22

home, but the house hadn't looked any different when Cass and all her brothers and sisters had lived there.

A feeling of contentment washed over her, the sort of feeling that can be brought on only by poignant memories and the smell of the old honeysuckle bush blooming outside the kitchen door. So many years of happiness had been spent in this house, and Cass suddenly realized how much she had missed being with her family.

Wylie came into the kitchen carrying Rosalee's youngest child and a round of excitement broke out as Cass viewed her newest nephew for the first time, then hugged her younger brother affectionately.

"I can't get over how much you've grown!" she exclaimed, holding him back away from her to get a closer look. He was at least five inches taller than when she had last seen him.

With a shy grin, Wylie mumbled some excuse about eating a lot, then quickly handed the baby to his grandmother. "I saw Luke drive in a while ago. I want to go see him."

"He's down at the barn with your dad," Neoma cautioned. "Don't get in their way."

"I won't!" Grabbing an apple from the bowl of fruit sitting on the buffet, he was out the door like a flash of lightning and on his way out the door.

"Well, I'm going to change the baby's diaper and get him settled down for a nap before I peel the potatoes for supper. Fix yourself a glass of tea, honey. I won't be long."

Neoma hustled out of the room while Cass went over to the cabinet to retrieve a glass. After she poured the drink she sat down at the table and waited for her mother to return.

She absently took a sip of the tea, trying to fight the small seed of curiosity that was beginning to grow inside her concerning Luke Travers. Funny, but she couldn't remember exactly what he looked like except he had blond hair and was sort of gangly.

When he had driven into the barnyard earlier she hadn't paid that much attention to who was behind the wheel of the truck so she didn't know if he had changed in looks. Probably not, unless he had just gotten homelier.

He had lived with his grandmother while he grew up because his parents had run off and left him. She remembered that much about him. The Travers's place was about three miles down the road from the Mc-Cason homestead, but she remembered her mom saying Minnie Travers had died a few years ago.

She looked out the window. I wonder if he still lives there? Her mom hadn't said anything about him being married, but that didn't mean he wasn't. As wild as he was, he had probably been herded to the altar by way of a double-barrel shotgun. Yes, he was probably married to one of the local girls and had several homely-looking kids running around the house. Pushing her glass back, she rose and glanced toward the door her mother had disappeared behind earlier. It would take a few minutes for her to get the baby settled. In the meantime maybe she should just run down and say hello to her dad.

Yes, it was all coming back to her now, she thought as she quickly slipped out the door and hurried down the path that led to the barn. She was only going to say hello to her father, not to see what that annoying Luke Travers looked like now.

She could almost guess.

He was probably still blond, gangly, and ugly as a mud fence. Undoubtedly age had improved neither his looks nor his disposition in the slightest.

CHAPTER TWO

Funny how time had such a way of being so fickle.

The familiar smells of hay and cattle surrounded her as she stood in the doorway for a moment trying to adjust her eyes to the dim interior of the building.

Uriah McCason was bent over a small heifer talking to her in soft, soothing tones while a younger man held the animal down and administered medicine with a syringe.

The calf's bellow was a weak, pitiful one as the elderly man continued to stroke the animal with a large, comforting hand. Uriah had been up since three that morning trying to save the calf, but there seemed to be little hope for its survival.

"Pop?"

With a weather-beaten face lined with fatigue and a lot more winkles than she had remembered, he turned his head to seek the sound of the voice that had called out to him. Standing in the shaft of sunlight, Uriah's eyesight, which was not as good as it once had been, could barely make out the slender form of his middle child, but when she called his name again he broke into a radiant smile.

"Cassie?"

"Yes, Pop. It's me."

"Well, come on over here, girl. Let me get a closer look at you."

Cassie stepped into the barn and walked over to her father, still amazed to see how he had aged in the time since she had last seen him. Why he must be nearing seventy, she thought with a jolt as he stood up and extended his arms out for her to come into.

Two bands of steel pulled her gruffly up against a broad chest that always smelled like sunshine and Red Man chewing tobacco, and his powerful grip belied the fact that Uriah McCason was no longer a young man.

She closed her eyes and returned the embrace with loving affection. "How are you, Pop?"

"I guess I'm doing okay for an old man. How's my Cassie girl?"

Uriah had always called her his "Cassie girl" and she smiled up at his tall six-foot-two stature and winked playfully. "Cassie girl's doin' great, Pop. Just great."

"So I've heard, so I've heard." Uriah held her back and inspected her with a critical parental eye. "Too skinny. Ain't got any meat on your bones at all. Don't they feed you up there in that big city?"

"Sure they do. And if you knew how hard I had to fight to stay 'skinny' you'd be ashamed for even mentioning it."

"Hogwash. You're goin' to make yourself sick if you don't start eatin'. Mom will have to fatten you up a little like she has your sisters. You'll never get a man lookin' like that."

"So who's having trouble getting a man?" she bantered with mock indignity.

"Luke, you remember our little Cassie, don't you?" Uriah put his arm around his daughter and turned her around to face the man who was still working quietly with the calf.

Six feet of solid muscle, thick dark blond hair with sunlightened streaks and a pair of the most arresting, cobalt-blue eyes Cass had ever encountered, glanced up and smiled politely at her.

Cassie had noticed that Luke, if indeed this was Luke Travers, had looked at her when she first came in, but then quickly turned his attention back to his work.

This man kneeling beside the calf was so ruggedly handsome it was almost impossible to associate him with the gangly, blond-headed boy of her youth. She just couldn't believe he had changed so much.

The man rose slowly to his feet, giving her another polite but distant smile.

His brilliant blue eyes met her gaze solidly. "Yes, I remember Cassie." He extended his hand. "It's been a while since you've been back."

No, it just couldn't be Luke Travers, she fretted as she tried to maintain her wavering facade. This man was too suave . . . too smooth . . . too . . . male. . . .

Whether it was from force of habit or just because he was Luke Travers, she suddenly felt her nose tilting upward with just the slightest hint of distaste as her hand was swallowed in his large one. "Yes. I live in New York and I don't get to make the trip back home as often as I would like," she acknowledged.

The way he had said "It's been a while since you've

28

been back" irritated her. It was almost like an accusation instead of a mere observance.

His eyes ran carelessly over her, taking in the designer silk dress and the string of cultured pearls she was wearing with cool detachment. The look wasn't insulting or even provocative, just inquisitive.

She felt resentment stir anew as she recognized the reserved, almost snooty look he had always managed to give her while they were busy ignoring each other in high school slowly come over his face as he withdrew a small cheroot out of his shirt pocket and stuck it between his even white teeth.

"That's what I hear." He cupped his hand to his lighter as he lit the small cigar. For a moment she thought he had completely dismissed her, but then he commented, "You work in some little office up there, don't you?"

He knew it was a poor choice of words, but he had intended it that way. She looked every bit as sassy as she had back in high school.

Her spine stiffened even more at the offhanded way he referred to her work. "I'm creative director of Creble and Associates," she corrected curtly. "It isn't a 'little office.' It happens to be a very big, highly successful advertising agency—on Madison Avenue." She doubted that would mean anything, but just in case it didn't, she wanted to enlighten. "You *have* heard of Madison Avenue?"

The blue of his eyes narrowed resentfully, then he smiled and conceded courteously, "Yes, I believe I have heard of Madison Avenue."

"Then you know that I don't work in a 'little office,' " she snapped.

He bowed his head in mock contrition. "Sorry. I stand corrected. *Big*"—he stressed the word obediently—"*highly* successful office in New York City."

She had to fight hard to keep the growing anger from showing on her face. "That's right."

Somehow they had both forgotten that Uriah was there watching this almost childish display of rudeness take place between them.

"Little office" indeed! Who did he think he was? Everyone in Rueter Flats knew how well Cass was doing and she would bet her bottom dollar Luke Travers knew it too. Well, she wasn't going to let him get under her skin. She was a little more mature than when they had been in high school together and she wouldn't allow him to irritate her this time.

She smiled at him, making it plain he was only something to be tolerated while they were in Uriah's presence. She literally forced civility back into her voice. "My goodness, it is so good to see you again. It's been a long time." Not long enough, but that was beside the point. "I understand you joined the service when I left for college."

"That's right." He reached over and picked up several instruments lying beside the calf and began to replace them in a brown leather bag.

"I hope they saved your job at the filling station," she remarked pleasantly. If he could be insulting, she could too. "A good grease monkey's hard to find."

"No, I gave it up when I decided to go to college," he remarked in an easy tone, then glanced up at her expectantly. "But I bought the service station a few years ago. You need gas?"

"No . . . I . . . I don't need gas. . . ."

"Oh. Well, when you run out, I'd be happy to tell Red to give you a discount while you're here." He went back to packing instruments while her pilot light went up another notch.

Damn! He'd *bought* the only gas station in Rueter Flats! If that wasn't enough to unnerve her, she still had to face the fact that he had gone to college too. She had always taken great pride in her degree, thinking that she was the only one in Rueter Flats who had one.

"You say you went to college?" she found herself probing in a decidedly petulant voice a few moments later.

"That's right."

"When?"

"A few months after I got out of the service." His first thought was to ignore the highfalutin little snit. She was baiting him and he knew it. He had seen her standing on the porch with her mother when he had driven up, decked out in her fancy designer clothes, lookin' as pretty as a Rocky Mountain sunrise. Neoma must have mentioned that he was the veterinarian coming to check on Uriah's sick calf.

His gaze skipped back over her broodingly. He had forgotten how damn good-looking she was and it rankled him to admit she looked every bit the part of the highly successful woman she was touted to be.

She had always been cute when they had been growing up, but she had become a real beauty. . . . He quickly shifted his attention back to his work. She might look good, but he'd bet his last dollar she was still the same old Cass McCason, by far the most ill-tempered little heifer he had ever met.

"Why, Luke's got him all kinds of degrees since you last seen him, honey." Uriah decided this had gone on long enough. He had to chuckle to himself. Two ornery kids! He would have thought that in the twelve years since they had seen each other they would have managed to outgrow all that childish animosity. "Like he mentioned, Uncle Sam put him through college right after he got out of the service and he's a veterinarian now." Uriah beamed at Luke proudly. "Not only that, but he runs his own ranch too. Got two thousand prime acres he has to look after on top of everything else."

Luke could tell that impressed her about as much as it would if she had stuck her high-priced fancy shoe in a pile of cow dung.

"Really." She tried to disguise her growing confusion. Luke's grandmother, Minnie Travers, had nothing but a run-down old farm when she had left years ago and Luke had been a juvenile delinquent still working at the local gas station.

Now all of a sudden he had a college degree, a reputable job, and a huge chunk of land Uriah was referring to as a "ranch," and . . . blond curly eyelashes that a woman would kill for. Not to mention other stunning assets. . . .

Well, it was too much. "What ranch?" she asked skeptically.

"Why, Luke took the acreage Minnie left him when she died and turned it into one of the finest cattle ranches around here. Didn't you see the big sign announcing THE SUNDOWNER when you drove into town?" Uriah exclaimed.

Yes, she had seen the sign. It had been quite impressive but she had never dreamed it belonged to anyone she knew, let alone Luke Travers. "Yes, I saw it. . . ." Her gaze reluctantly crept back up to meet Luke's amused one. "Is that yours?"

A slow, extremely aggravating grin spread lazily across his face now as his blue gaze met hers almost triumphantly. "My, how times are a changin', huh?"

She slumped against a bale of hay and sat there for a moment just looking at him.

Luke Travers could probably buy and sell her three times over.

It was hard to swallow.

"That's very nice," she finally managed. "I never realized your grandmother had so much land."

"She always had the land. She was just never inclined to run cattle on it."

"And you are?"

His smile still held that edge of cockiness. "Yes, I've acquired a few head."

Uriah nearly choked on that one. A "few" head consisted of at least fifteen hundred of the best beef cattle around. "Well, I'll bet Mom's got supper almost on the table," Uriah intervened brightly. "I'll have her set another place if you can stay, Luke."

Luke gathered up the remaining instruments and prepared to depart. "Thanks, Uriah, I hate to miss one of Neoma's meals, but I'll have to pass. I have another stop to make on the way home."

"You sure, boy? I think I smelled pot roast when I went in earlier," he tempted.

There was no doubt that Neoma's tender pot roast, swimming in rich brown gravy, was Luke's favorite, but the temptation was quickly overcome when he glanced at Cassie and saw the look of sheer relief cross her face when he declined the offer.

For a brief, devilish moment, Luke considered retracting his refusal and accepting her father's offer just to see her squirm, but then thought better of it.

He didn't care for her company any more than she cared for his.

"Sounds good, Uriah, but I'm afraid I'll have to make it another time," he apologized again.

"Well, sure, but now you are going to be at the party for Cassie Saturday night, aren't you?" Cassie tried to motion to Uriah that it didn't matter, but he seemed persistent in getting an answer out of Luke.

"Can't really say," Luke hedged. "I'll keep it in mind, though."

That still wasn't good enough for Uriah. When Cassie came home he wanted all his friends there to welcome her. "At least promise you'll drop by, even if you can't stay long."

Luke chuckled as he realized he wasn't going to be let off the hook. "Okay. I'll stop by sometime during the evening," he relented.

He meticulously avoided looking at her.

And she went out of her way to avoid looking at him.

"Where's Wylie?" It suddenly dawned on her that her little brother wasn't in the barn.

"He was here a while earlier but he decided to go down to the pond and fish before supper," Uriah answered. "Guess one of us ought to go down and get him."

"Don't hold out too much hope on the calf," Luke

34

cautioned again as the three of them walked out of the barn. "The odds are against her making it."

"Yes," Uriah sighed. "I was afraid she wouldn't. I hate to lose her, sort of got attached to the little booger, but I'll see that she's comfortable." Uriah had lost many a calf over the years and it still never failed to bother him. He glanced toward the pond thoughtfully. "Cassie, you take Luke up to the house and get him something cold to drink before he leaves. I'll go get the boy."

She would much rather go after Wylie, but she didn't want it to seem obvious so she managed to sound almost cordial when she agreed. "Okay, Pop."

Uriah broke off and walked in the direction of the pond as Luke and Cassie proceeded to the house.

At first neither one made an attempt at conversation. Cassie was intent on trying to keep up with Luke's long-legged strides and Luke was intent on ignoring her.

But the house was a small distance from the barn so Cassie decided to at least be sociable. "Mom says you and Wylie have become good friends."

"Yeah, he's a good kid," Luke complimented.

They walked on in silence and a few moments later she tried again. "It's good of you to take your free time and spend it with Wylie. Do you have children of your own now?"

Now why did she ask that! He would think she was trying to pry into his personal affairs!

But if he thought her remark was out of context, he didn't show it. Instead, he kept on walking, his eyes straight ahead. "No, I don't have any children of my own."

35

She spoke before she thought. "You mean that you know about," she teased, then was horrified she had been so crass.

For a moment his pace slackened and he turned to focus a very frosty, highly indignant blue gaze squarely on her. "No," he stated again, pronouncing the word so emphatically that even a one-year-old could have understood him. "I'm quite sure I do not have any children—anywhere."

She felt her face redden like a prairie fire. "Pardon me," she apologized in the same tone he was using with her. "I was only teasing."

His gaze flicked over her coolly one more time, then he turned and started walking again.

She decided to forget the sociable bit. It wasn't working. As they approached the backyard of the farmhouse their eyes fell on the shiny new Jaguar sitting next to the well house.

"That's mine," Cassie announced as she watched his eyes run over the car appreciatively.

"That would have been my first guess."

"It's a Jaguar," she taunted, ashamed she was being so repulsive, yet unable to stop herself.

"I know what it is. We have picture books here in Rueter Flats."

She looked at him sourly. "Pretty nice, huh?" She had no idea why she was baiting him like she was. He could probably buy a Jaguar just as easy as she could, yet she'd bet anything that he would try and pretend indifference to the car.

People around Rueter Flats might have books with pictures in them, but they sure didn't see a Jaguar every day of their lives.

But to her surprise he was relatively nice about his answer. "Yes, it is nice. Is it new?"

"Almost. I bought it six months ago."

He walked around the car, inspecting it closer. "It has a scratch on the right front fender," he informed calmly as he circled back to stand beside her.

Cassie frowned when she remembered the rock her nephew had thrown earlier. "Oh, I know. Bobby Ray threw a rock at the dog and it was standing in front of the car," she complained.

"Well"—Luke started for the house again, leaving her standing beside the car rubbing at the scratch irritably—"if you're going to spend your money on a Jaguar, you'd better learn to take care of it."

"I do!" She objected to that! "It didn't have a scratch on it before I came here."

He looked as if he doubted that, but he wisely decided to let the issue drop. "While you're here you might take it over to Dave Levell's garage. You remember him, don't you? He went to school with us during our senior year."

She remembered. Dave had never had the sense to get in out of the rain, let alone work on an expensive car.

"Yes, I remember Dave. Don't tell me you actually let him work on your cars."

"Yes, he's done some work for me in the past," Luke relayed offhandedly. "And he's darn good."

"Well, thanks, but I'll wait until I get back to New York," she said with a final swipe at the angry scratch.

Dave Levell might be good enough to work on Luke's old heaps, but she sure didn't want some local yokel working on her Jag.

"It was only a suggestion," Luke dismissed mildly.

He stepped up on the porch while she still trailed a few feet behind him. Seconds later the screen door banged loudly shut in her face.

Well! she seethed, then angrily jerked the door back open.

This was the same old Luke Travers she remembered!

CHAPTER THREE

When Uriah and Neoma gave a party folks would come from miles around. The McCasons would shove the furniture out of the way and the entire house would be opened up to their friends and relatives. There would be enough food and drink to feed a small army, and the dancing would go on long past midnight. Such was the occasion of Cassie's homecoming and celebration party the following Saturday night.

Cassie grumbled under her breath as she stood before the mirror in her bedroom and frowned at her reflection. It was going to be impossible to make her hair look decent in this wilting humidity. Uriah had never invested in air-conditioning, so consequently the house was still like a steam oven from the day's heat. She could have literally wrung the water out of the air, and every time she created a bouncy, long, dark brunet curl with her iron, it fell right back out again.

"Lordy, lordy, the place is really beginning to fill up and I'm about to melt." Rachel burst through the doorway and hurried over to the bed and flopped down comfortably, cradling her infant child in her arms. "The baby's hungry. You don't mind if I feed him up here while we talk, do you?"

39

"Of course not. Go right ahead. I'm just trying to do something with my hair." Her sister Rachel was as pretty as she had been in high school, even though that was four babies and eleven years ago. She had the same dark hair and brown eyes as her other sisters, and she had always been the bubbly, vivacious one of the family.

"Your hair always looks so pretty," she praised as she began mechanically to unbutton her blouse. "But then you're pretty all over."

Cassie grinned at the lovely compliment while her eyes were unwillingly drawn to the ritual of Rachel breast-feeding her child. Her sister's eyes radiated with love as she fed the child. Cassie knew it was the way God intended for an infant to be fed, yet the whole process left her feeling a little uneasy. It looked—quite painful, actually.

"Doesn't that hurt?" she asked as the baby sucked noisily for a few moments.

"No, not at all. Who does your hair?" Rachel changed the subject momentarily.

"Oh, a man by the name of Stephan." Cassie picked up the curling iron again and wrapped it tightly around another strand of hair.

Rachel closed her eyes dreamily, trying to envision what it would be like to have a man named Stephan cut her hair. "Stephan. That sounds real nice. What's that style called?" she asked.

"I'm not sure. It's something Stephan does exclusively." Cass surveyed the tapered sides, not at all sure she liked them. Somehow it lacked the sophistication she was striving for.

"It's real nice," Rachel praised once more. "Your hair's gettin' real long. I like it that way."

"Thanks, it's easy to care for—usually. Where do you go when you get your hair cut?" Cassie asked conversationally.

Rachel sighed. "I usually cut it myself. Nellie Sooter's the only one around here who has a beauty shop."

Cassie lifted one brow disdainfully. "Nellie Sooter? Why she must be eighty years old by now."

"Yeah, eighty-two," Rachel said wistfully. "She gave me a permanent last summer that Jesse said looked like I had run into a high-voltage wire." She giggled. "Took me three months to grow it all out. Since then I do my own."

Cassie shook her head in disgust at the lack of services offered in Rueter Flats as she released the curling iron and the curl fell flat on her head once more.

Her brown eyes flashed angrily. "Cripes!" She threw the iron back on the dresser and unplugged it. "I can't do anything with this mop!"

"Don't need nothing done to it," Rachel assured. "It looks good, Cass. Real good." Rachel picked up the baby and put him over her shoulder to pat his back gently as Cass strolled over to the closet to select what she would wear for the evening. The customary denims and Western shirt usually worn at these informal gatherings would be far too hot in this heat. She thumbed through her clothing and finally withdrew a lightweight skirt and matching blouse in a pretty shade of red.

"What do you think about this?" Cass held the ensemble against her and studied herself critically in the

41

mirror. The simple cotton creation was her newest purchase and this would be the first time she had worn it.

"It's truly lovely," Rachel sighed as she settled the baby to her other breast. "It's such a pretty color."

"It's called summer red," Cass murmured absently as she carefully studied her selection, then decided it wouldn't be too dressy.

She began to dress and their conversation drifted off to earlier days when they had shared this room together. The same wallpaper—bright splotches of red and yellow flowers—still adorned the wall, and the double bed with the yellow chenille bedspread still had its place in the middle of the room.

They laughed over the stories of lost loves and of the dreams they used to share together while they were trying to get to sleep at night, and both agreed those times were some of the happiest ones in their lives.

"Oh, I know it's wishful thinking, but I sure wish you lived back home again," Rachel sighed. "We used to have such good times. We miss you, Cass. The whole family does."

"And I miss all of you, but New York is my home now," Cass reasoned as she sat down on the side of the bed to tie the matching, mid-heel ankle pump she had just slipped on.

"I know it is," Rachel conceded with that same touch of wistfulness in her voice. "But I was hoping you had sorta got your fill of the big city and was ready to come home now. You know, Pop's health isn't what it used to be."

At the mention of her father's health Cass frowned. "What's wrong with Pop? He looks fine to me."

"Oh, nothing in particular," Rachel comforted. "It's just, I don't know. He just doesn't seem to have the bounce he used to have."

"Well, he's almost seventy," Cass pointed out gently as she slid off the bed and walked back to stand before the mirror. "I imagine we'll lose some of our bounce by the time we reach that age."

"I suppose so, still . . ." Rachel's voice trailed off undecidedly. "I guess I just can't stand the thought of Mom and Pop getting old."

Cass laughed softly. "I know. But I think that's only natural."

"Yes, I guess so. You really don't think you'll ever come back here?" Rachel's eyes held a faint glimmer of hope, even though she knew Rueter Flats would never hold a candle to New York City in Cassie's eyes.

"No." Cassie smiled, hoping to cushion her disappointment. "I don't think so. I have my work there and it's important to me."

"Can't really blame you," Rachel conceded as the baby finished his dinner and she rebuttoned her blouse. "Not much to attract you around here. Not even many eligible men unless it would be Luke Travers or Seth Holoson or Bray Williams."

Her grin turned defiantly wicked as she watched her sister for the reaction she knew would soon be coming at the mention of Luke. Cassie had never particularly cared for Luke, strange as that might be. Rachel had always thought he was exciting, a real free spirit.

Cassie picked up her blusher and dabbed it irritably on her cheeks. "Luke Travers would be the last reason I would come back," she said curtly.

"Yeah, I know, but I bet you were a little surprised

to see how good-lookin' he is now." Rachel's grin widened. "Not that he wasn't always nice-looking, but since he's gotten older . . ."

"I've seen him only once since I got home, but he looks like the same old Luke to me," Cassie snapped, but she felt her hand involuntarily hesitating as her memory conjured up Luke's virile good looks.

Well, perhaps not exactly the same, and yes, she had been surprised at his vast improvement, but then men's looks always seem to enhance with age.

"Luke's about the best catch around here," Rachel insisted. "Seth's all right, but Bray's gettin' a little old and crotchety. I think he'll probably be a bachelor all his life. But now that ole Luke, he has all the available girls absolutely swooning over him, not to mention all the unavailable ones," she giggled.

"Good for ole Luke, but this is one who'll never swoon over him." Cassie pitched the blusher down on the dresser and reached for a small bottle of perfume.

"He still rankles you a little, doesn't he?"

"Me? Heaven's no. Until I came home day before yesterday I hadn't given Luke Travers a thought since we were in high school together."

"I think you're still mad at him because he took Sybil Wilson to that dance instead of you," Rachel heckled playfully.

Now that was really the last straw. Cassie whirled around to face Rachel defensively. "What a thing to say, Rachel Murdock! I didn't actually want Luke to take me to that dance!"

"You did too." Rachel said matter-of-factly. She was absolutely sure her memory served her correctly. "I remember it like it was yesterday. We were all

44

standing around after school one day and the subject of the Friday-night dance was brought up. Luke asked you if you had a date and you mistakenly thought he was asking you for a date."

Cassie felt her face flood with color. "I wouldn't have gone to a dog fight with Luke Travers," she denied sheepishly, but she did remember the incident and it had been highly embarrassing.

Luke had asked her if she had a date in front of all their friends. She didn't have a date and at the time she theorized it would be better to go to the dance with Luke than not go at all.

After all, not every one in town despised him quite the way she did. Some of the girls she ran around with foolishly thought he was "cute." But not her. She would only be going with him so she wouldn't have to show up without a date. But he had promptly made it known he was only asking if she had a date out of curiosity, that he was planning on asking that wild Sybil Wilson to go with him.

Well, that was only fitting. They were both as fast as New York cab drivers.

"That's not the way I remember it," Rachel persisted until Cassie was forced to shoot her a highly annoyed reminder that she was getting tired of the subject.

"Oh, my." Rachel quickly heeded the familiar warning signal and quickly jumped up to investigate the tantalizing fragrance Cassie was irritably dabbing behind her ears. "What's that wonderful smell?"

Cassie was relieved to hear that Rachel was going to finally drop the subject of Luke Travers. Strange how mention of that long-ago incident with Luke still had the power to annoy her. "It's called Giorgio." She held the bottle out for Rachel to get a better whiff.

Rachel inhaled the rich scent appreciatively. "Smells real expensive. Jesse got me a bottle of Windsong for my birthday and I thought it was just about the nicest thing I'd ever smelled, but this would just fairly take your breath away."

Cassie smiled and brushed a small amount behind Rachel's ear. "Go find Jesse and see what he thinks of it."

"He'll die, he'll just die," Rachel exclaimed, inhaling deeply of the intoxicating scent floating around the room.

Cass didn't know if she had done her sister a favor or not. More than likely another resident of Rueter Flats would be on its way by tomorrow morning, she thought ruefully as Rachel happily scurried out of the room to find her husband.

Casting one last critical eye in the mirror, she decided she would have to do.

Besides, she wasn't out to impress anyone. It would just be the same old friends and neighbors she had known since she was a baby at the party tonight.

Luke Travers suddenly appeared back in her thoughts and she shrugged him away immediately.

And she had not wanted to go to that dance with him, she denied emphatically to the mirror once more. Swiping up a tube of lip gloss, she applied it to her lips with swift, efficient movements. And if he was the best catch in four counties, then the poor women of Rueter Flats were fishing in the wrong hole.

* * *

The party was in full swing when she came down the stairway five minutes later. Several of the men had brought their guitars, banjos, and fiddles and they were standing in the corner of the living room tuning up their instruments.

A murmur went up as she stepped into the parlor.

She was immediately greeted by a sea of friendly faces crowding around, all wanting to talk to her at the same time. As she passed through the crowd exchanging hugs and handshakes, she soon became caught up in the festivities of the occasion. Everyone wanted to tell her how good it was to have her home and congratulate her on her upcoming promotion with Creble and Associates.

"Tom and Karen! It's wonderful to see you again," she exclaimed as she shook hands with a couple of her former classmates. "And this can't be little Jacob?"

A beaming child of around six years old stared up at her angelically as she paused and patted the top of his curly brown head.

"Yeah, can you believe how he's growin'?" Karen said proudly.

"It's hard to comprehend. He's going to be as tall as his dad if he keeps on at this rate," Cass praised.

At six foot five, two hundred and fifty pounds, Tom Metsker had always been an imposing sight in the community and it looked as if his son was following in his footsteps. Cass eyed Karen teasingly. "I thought by now Jacob would have another brother or sister to play with."

The look Tom and Karen exchanged was a tender

one and Cass immediately realized she had hit upon a touchy subject.

"Oh, we've been tryin' real hard," Karen murmured.

"Just don't seem to have much luck," Tom confessed with a soft chuckle as he took his wife's hand and squeezed it lovingly.

It always came as a surprise for Cass to hear such a nice soft voice come out of such a large man.

Cass reached out to pat her hand reassuringly. "Well, I'm sure one of these days you'll hear the patter of little feet racing through the house."

"I sure hope so," Karen sighed. "Isn't it just wonderful about Rosalee?"

"Yes, Ray seems to be real excited about becoming a father again," Cass agreed, then excused herself a few moments later and moved on through the crowd.

An hour later she was out of breath and her face flushed happily with exertion as she danced first one and then another dance with the men of Rueter Flats. Some were eligible, some were married, and some were nearing eighty years old, but she found herself enjoying the old-fashioned clogging with each and every one of them.

She had been raised on Saturday-night dances just like this one, but she hadn't realized how much she had missed them.

There was just something about briskly two steppin' around the crowded floor to a fast-paced tune that the chic discos in New York couldn't quite compare with.

Around ten another murmur went up in the crowd as Cass was standing at the punch bowl with a former classmate, Seth Holoson. They had just danced the last two dances and decided to sit the next one out. Seth handed her a cup of punch as she glanced over to the doorway to see what all the excitement was about.

With a frown, she saw Luke enter the room.

Moments later he was surrounded by every eligible woman in the room from sixteen to sixty. She watched with utter amazement as they fluttered around him and, in her eyes, made absolute fools of themselves.

"There's Luke Travers," Seth remarked needlessly as he tilted his cup up and took a drink of the cold liquid. "You remember ole Luke, don't you?"

"Yes." Cass turned her eyes back to Seth and smiled. "I remember ole Luke." Even on the remote possibility she had forgotten him, everyone she had come in contact with since she returned home seemed bent on jogging her memory when it came to Luke Travers.

She turned her attention back to Seth and they made idle conversation for a few moments as they stood and drank their punch. Cass was determined to ignore the latecomer. By arriving as late as he had, she was well aware this was Luke's devious little way of stating he was there only in deference to Uriah, not to celebrate Cass's homecoming.

Well so what, she thought. He doesn't bother me one little bit. But when her mind repeatedly refused to focus on what Seth was saying, she realized with growing frustration that as bad as she hated to admit it, it did bother her.

He was a stunning man, much as it irked her to acknowledge that, and men didn't usually give her such a cold shoulder. Especially not at her own party!

It was downright degrading for him to deliberately ignore her this way.

Her gaze involuntarily found its way back across the room and paused once more. What did he have that had all those silly women in such a dither? Was it the way his pants fit snugly to his muscled thighs, or that his chest was uncommonly broad, or that his waist was sleekly trim? She quickly snapped her head back around. Get a hold of yourself, Cassie! He's just a man, for heaven's sake!

It irritated her to think that it was quite possible Luke was one of those men who took the ladies' breath away and wasn't even aware of what he was doing. Of all the things she could accuse him of, and they were many and varied, being stuck on himself had never been one of his faults—but of course up until now he had no reason to be.

He was dressed casually tonight, in denims and a red plaid shirt. He was wearing an attractive honey-colored leather vest that made his hair look even blonder. As he had entered the room he had taken off a large Stetson and handed it to one of the young teenage girls to take care of.

The girl had giggled with delight and Cass could almost see the excited way her heart had fluttered when he winked at her playfully.

He should be ashamed of himself for tantalizing a girl that age, she thought reproachfully, then carefully forced her attention back to Seth.

But try as she would, Luke's appearance put a damper on her evening. Oh, he didn't bother her personally. On the contrary, he ignored her as steadfastly as she ignored him. Even when they danced past each other they carefully turned their heads in opposite directions.

She had to allow him one concession, though. He had good taste in his women. The girl he had been dancing with for the last hour was a real looker and they made a striking couple.

She was petite, with platinum-blond hair and an ivory complexion like one of those Kewpie dolls Cassie had won at the fair one year. He was tall and tanned, with golden hair and twinkling blue eyes.

The girl wasn't familiar to Cass, but then there were a lot of unfamiliar faces in the crowd tonight. Whoever she was, it was clear she didn't view Luke with the same distaste that Cass did.

Once more she deliberately forced her attention elsewhere. Still, to her utter dismay, the next half hour found her eyes constantly searching the room to see where he was and what he was doing.

Finally, a little before midnight, she gave up trying to ignore his presence and slipped quietly out the back door for a much-needed breath of fresh air.

A huge, round moon hung suspended over her head as she began to stroll toward the corral. Its silvery beams lit her path. The air was richly perfumed with the scent of honeysuckle as she wandered over to the fence and paused. One of the horses neighed softly and ambled over to where she stood.

"Hi there, girl." Cassie rubbed the mare's nose affectionately.

The horse whinnied low and nuzzled deeper into the palm of her hand looking for a treat.

"No sugar cubes tonight, but I'll bring you one tomorrow," she promised.

51

A low, grunting sound caught her ear and her gaze was drawn to where her car sat down by the barn.

Because of the party, Uriah had suggested she park the Jaguar out of the way so the party guests would have plenty of room for their cars and trucks.

The bright moonbeams made the little sports car glisten like a rare jewel in a nest of black velvet, and once again a feeling of pride overcame her.

The car was the nicest thing she had ever had, and it made her feel good to know that she had worked hard to earn it. Not that it was all hers—yet. But it would be in thirty-six more payments.

Once more the strange, grunting sound reached her ears and she could have sworn she saw the car rock back and forth.

Giving the horse one final pat, she began to edge toward the barn, a puzzled frown on her face now.

A loud snort rent the air and her eyes widened as she stepped backward a fraction. She paused and listened for a moment, then began to move forward again. She couldn't imagine what was going on because the noise sounded exactly like one of Uriah's old sows grunting—but that would be impossible. It was nearly midnight and the pigs were all asleep.

But to her growing puzzlement the noise sounded again and the car definitely moved this time.

Stepping around the vehicle, her mouth dropped open in outrage as she saw a huge pig rubbing up and down on the front bumper, grunting with contentment as it calmly scratched itself back and forth, back and forth. . . .

It must have weighed close to five hundred pounds,

and each movement caused the small car to vibrate up and down in a most unnerving manner.

"Good grief!" Cassie squealed about the same time the old sow did, and the still night air exploded. "What do you think you're doing!" she demanded. "Shoo! Shoo! Get out of here!" She bolted toward the sow as it shrieked frantically and went down on the ground for a minute before it could gain enough traction to jump back up and run.

She was flinging her arms at the animal, yelling, enraged to think that the Jaguar would have yet more damage done to it. At the rate things were going, she would have to take her car back to New York in a brown paper sack!

An enraged Cassie, hot on the heels of a terrified pig, came racing around the car just in time to run head-on into the solid wall of a man's chest.

The pig squealed again and ducked between his legs while Cassie slammed into his chest like a bullet. For a moment it looked as if they were both going down, but the man finally managed to steady both of them.

"What in the . . . !"

Cassie caught her breath and looked up into familiar blue eyes and her heart sank. Oh, brother. It would have to be him! He had undoubtedly seen the whole fiasco with the pig and her car and no doubt he would have a field day laughing behind her back and telling the humiliating story.

Still so mad she could barely speak, she drew herself up indignantly and stepped back from him, her brown eyes sizzling like a hot bed of coals.

"You—he—that darn pig—rubbed on my bumper and left pig hairs and now I have a scratch and no

53

telling what else. . . . Oh, you! . . . I thought pigs were supposed to sleep at night!" She broke off when she realized she was literally yelling at Luke as if it was all his fault and jabbing at the pig, who was now heading full speed toward the barn lot.

Luke was looking at her as if she had lost her mind. He had been on his way to the barn to check the sick calf again before he left for home when he had heard all the commotion.

To her mortification she burst into tears and began sobbing. She knew she should have stayed home this year! "Oh—you—don't you dare repeat this to anyone!" she warned as she shook her finger threateningly under his nose, then marched angrily off in the direction of the house.

To her further humiliation she felt one of the heels on her new shoes snap like a broken bone. Gritting her teeth with pure rage, she reached down and picked up the broken heel and, further enraged, hurled it at Luke's head.

With a look of sheer disbelief, he hurried ducked as it went sailing past his ear. He cautiously straightened back up in time to watch her storm off to the house in a real snit, still trying to figure out what she had been so hysterical and mad at him about.

Whatever it was, it apparently concerned her fancy car, and whatever had happened, she deserved it for being so uppity!

He had been right all along. She was still the meanest little heifer he knew.

CHAPTER FOUR

A vacation was supposed to be a restful time, a time when one had nothing to do but loll around and dread the thought of going back to work, but Cassie's vacation had been the exact opposite.

She had been so busy running around seeing old friends and visiting in the homes of each brother and sister during her brief stay that she had barely had time to catch her breath.

Returning home late Tuesday afternoon after an extended shopping session with Rosalee and her children, Cassie rushed up to her room and kicked off her shoes, stripped down to her slip and panties, then flopped down on the bed with a sigh of relief. The bed felt like sheer heaven.

She hadn't known a day could be so long!

Shopping in Macon seemed like such a good idea at first. Cassie was thrilled that she was able to take her nephews out and buy them each a shiny new pair of leather cowboy boots. Of course the baby wasn't quite ready for boots yet, so a tiny pair of Nikes was purchased for him.

Cassie loved to see the way their eyes lit up as they preened proudly in the shoe-store mirror, announcing for all those who cared to listen that their Aunt Cassie had bought the shoes for them!

But the newness of the shopping expedition wore off quickly and the children had become fussy and hard to get along with.

Hoping that a good lunch would improve their dispositions, Cassie treated them all. The meal did nothing to restore the children's good nature, but Rosalee enjoyed the unaccustomed luxury so much that at least Cassie felt better.

By the time they had finished wiping hands, scraping macaroni and cheese off tiny faces, and digging smashed green beans from beneath clenched fingers, Cassie was beginning to see the folly of her earlier suggestion.

"I want a thucker now!" Bobby Ray demanded.

Cassie glanced at Rosalee. "Can he have a 'thucker,' Mom?"

"Oh, sure," Rosalee consented blithely, and Cassie had to wonder if she had considered what they were going to do with all the sticky faces and hands.

But it was when the baby decided to do his "thing" as they were pushing his stroller through the crowded maze that Cassie knew the shopping spree had been a horrendous mistake. Of course about this time the two older boys quickly decided they needed to use the public facilities, too, so Cassie was forced to halfheartedly offer to change Joey Ray's diaper while Rosalee assisted the two older ones.

Several times she was sure she would gag herself to death before she finished the awesome task of getting a clean diaper on Joey Ray, but fifteen minutes later she was tucking him neatly back into his stroller with a sigh of relief.

By now Billy Ray and Bobby Ray had every hand dryer in the room blowing full blast and Cassie's head was pounding like an African war drum.

The rest of the afternoon had been a blur of sticky hands and more dirty diapers, and Cassie had never been so glad to finally call it a day.

If a vacation was what she had wanted, she would have to hurry and get back to work, she thought dryly as she closed her eyes and luxuriated in the glorious silence.

And to top it all off, her throat was beginning to bother her again. This past winter had found her with a sore throat more often than not, but she had hoped that with summer's arrival she would finally have a reprieve.

Oh well, day after tomorrow she would get in her Jag and head back to New York. When she got back home she would see her doctor and the sore throat would disappear for another few weeks.

Thank goodness vacation would be over for another year.

But she honestly didn't know how Rosalee kept her sanity.

She must have been more exhausted than she realized because the next thing she knew Neoma was gently shaking her shoulder to awaken her for dinner.

"Supper's on the table, hon."

Raising sleep-filled eyes, Cassie murmured something about not being hungry and tugged the pillow over her head.

Neoma chuckled softly and pulled the corner of the

spread up over her gently. It wouldn't hurt to let her sleep a little longer. Uriah had eaten early and driven into Macon for a meeting, and Wylie had gone to a baseball game with Luke, so it would just be her and Cassie eating together tonight anyway.

Her hand reached out and tenderly touched the wisps of dark hair that fell around her daughter's face, a loving smile touching the corners of her mouth now. Cassie looked like she did when she was a child. Her face was warm and flushed with sleep and she looked so very young and innocent to Neoma.

When Cassie had first moved to New York, Neoma had spent many a restless night lying beside Uriah, both of them tossing with worry about their daughter's welfare. But Cassie had made it fine. She had made them all proud, and Neoma had to admit that she was no longer a child. She was a lovely woman now, and Neoma was so glad to have her back home for a while. She sighed softly, then turned and slipped quietly out of the room. She would keep a plate warm and she could eat when she got up.

But when she returned a couple of hours later, Cassie was still sleeping as soundly as before. A small seed of concern began to take root as she bent over her daughter and once more nudged her shoulder.

"Cassie, you'd better wake up, dear. You won't sleep a wink tonight if you don't."

Cassie could hear her mom's voice calling from somewhere far away, but the warm cocoon of sleep that had enveloped her was reluctant to release her from its pleasant hold.

"Cassie?" Neoma was becoming more than a little concerned now. It wasn't at all like Cassie to sleep this long in the afternoon. "Cassie. Can you hear me? Wake up!"

Her mom's voice was sharply insistent this time and Cass tried to force her eyes to unlock. "What?" she murmured drowsily. Her mouth felt dry and hot and she was vaguely aware of a deepening ache in her throat.

"Goodness." Neoma heaved a sigh of relief and sat down on the edge of the bed. "I was beginning to get worried about you."

"Worried? Why?" Cassie rolled over and tried to focus her gaze on her mother but seemed to have a hard time doing so.

"You didn't want to wake up, and that's not like you at all."

"Yes . . . I know. . . . I'm just so tired. . . ." She swallowed and the action proved to be extremely painful. Her right hand shot up to touch her throat. "My throat hurts," she complained.

"It does?" Neoma's hand immediately went to her daughter's forehead and she frowned. "Land's sake, Cassie. You're burnin' up with fever."

"I am?" The news was more than a little disturbing. If her throat was this sore and she was running a fever again, it could only mean that she was in for another bout of tonsillitis. Twice in the past few months she had missed several days of work due to the annoying recurrence. "Surely not. I was feeling fine earlier."

"It sure feels like it to me, but there's a sure way to find out." Neoma slid off the bed and went in search of a thermometer. Moments later she was back, shaking the mercury down as she walked. "Have your tonsils been bothering you again lately?"

"Every once in a while," Cassie admitted as she obediently opened her mouth and Neoma peered into her throat.

"Oh, my."

Cassie's heart sank. Neoma had said that in the glum, tsking way mothers have that assure you you're in for big trouble. Shaking her head worriedly, she placed the thermometer under her daughter's tongue.

"We should have had those things out long ago," Neoma fused as she plumped the pillow and clucked like the typical mother. "Doc warned us that you were going to have nothing but trouble if you didn't."

"I know." Cassie had heard that a hundred times, but she cringed when she thought about having the operation at her age. A sudden chill assaulted her and she began to shiver uncontrollably as Neoma hurried over to the closet and withdrew a couple of lightweight blankets to drape over her. The room was at least eighty degrees but Cassie felt it had suddenly dropped to below zero.

"Tha-n-kk-s, M-om." She was barely able to talk now as intermittent chills shook her slender frame.

"Dear, dear," Neoma twittered worriedly. "I think I'd better go call Doc Lydell and see if he can run over here."

Any other time Cassie would have voiced a stern protest, but she had been through tonsillitis enough to know that she would have to have an antibiotic to get over it. Simple aspirin wouldn't do this time. "I think you'd better," she agreed, then huddled down deeper into the blanket.

But a few minutes later Neoma was back with bad news. "He's not home. Mildred said he had surgery over in Macon today and she doesn't know what time he'll get back. He may even spend the night over there if the patient doesn't do well."

"Well, it's not exactly an emergency," Cassie pointed out around the thermometer, which was still stuck in her mouth like an ice pick. "Just give me a couple of aspirins and we'll call him in the morning."

Withdrawing the thermometer, Neoma's brow furrowed deeper. "I don't think we should wait till mornin'. You have a hundred and four temperature."

"It's been that high before."

"I don't care. That's dangerous for an adult to have that high a temperature. Uriah will have to drive you over to the emergency room in Macon. Doc Lydell will surely still be there. I don't want to take the chance that the fever will go any higher."

"Mom, really—"

"Oh, dear!"

Cassie's head shot up from beneath her pile of blankets. "What?"

"Your father's not back yet—he went to a Grange meetin' tonight. . . . Well, I'll just call Ray to come and take you," she decided.

"Rosalee said Ray had to go to a deacons' meeting at the church tonight," Cassie murmured.

"Oh, my stars, that's right. Then I'll call Pauly—"

"Pauly and Newt have gone fishing."

"Oh, dear me." Neoma sank down on the bed in dismay, realizing that Cassie was right. Pauly and Newt had stopped by earlier and borrowed some of Uriah's tackle before they went on down to the river. She reached over to feel her daughter's forehead again. "You're hotter."

"No, I'm not."

"Yes, you are."

"No, I'm not."

"Don't argue with me. You're hotter than a two-dollar pistol."

The sound of a truck pulling into the graveled drive finally broke the impasse as Neoma sprang to her feet and rushed to the window. "Thank goodness. It's Luke bringing Wylie home," she announced with a rush of relief. "He can take you to Macon."

"Mom!" But before Cassie could stop her, Neoma had spun on her heel and left the room in a flurry of excitement. With a disgusted moan, Cassie jerked the blankets up over her head and scrunched lower in the bed. All she needed to top a perfectly miserable day was Luke Travers's company!

But with much to-do about nothing, Neoma returned a few minutes later dragging a puzzled Luke along behind her. "She's right in here, Luke. She's being ornery, but I want you to take a look at her and see what you think."

He paused in the doorway, his gaze quickly locating Cassie, who was lying in the middle of the bed vibrating like half-set Jell-O.

She felt her face growing even hotter with embarrassment as he eased cautiously over to her bedside.

"What's going on?" he asked quietly.

Neoma had run out of the house yelling at him just as he had dropped Wylie off and started to pull out of the drive. She had babbled something about Cassie needing a doctor and he'd better get upstairs quick!

Cassie made an apologetic face. "Mom is overreacting a little."

He stepped closer to the side of her bed to examine her flushed features more accurately. "How high's your fever?"

"I'll bet it's shot even higher than it was when I took it a while ago," Neoma fretted. "You're a doctor, Luke. Tell her she's taking a chance if she waits until morning to get some medicine."

"Mother." Cassie shot her an annoyed look. "Luke is a veterinarian, not a people doctor."

"Well, I'll bet there ain't a whole lot of difference, is there?" Neoma prompted hopefully to Luke.

"Nope, dealing with one jackass is just about like dealing with another," Luke agreed, with just the suggestion of a grin on his face for her mother's sake. He leaned over the bed. "Open your mouth, Cass, and let me have a look."

"I will not!" This was beginning to get ridiculous. She wasn't about to let him peer into her throat!

"Don't give me a hard time," he warned with the familiar edge of impatience he always used when addressing her.

"Don't give me one. I said no."

"Fine with me," he said indifferently, and promptly stepped back from the bed. "She won't let me look in her throat, Neoma."

He sounded exactly like he was tattling on her!

"Now, children," Neoma pacified. "This is not the time to be ugly to one another. Now, Cassie. You sit up there and let Luke look at your throat," she ordered in a tone that Cassie knew meant business.

It was quite unnerving to be ordered around like a child again, but Cassie began to slide back up from the depths of the blankets and glare at Luke hostilely.

"This is a waste of time. I don't need you to look in my throat and tell me I'm sick! I know I am, but Doc Lydell is out of town and I don't want to have to go clear over to Macon tonight to see him."

Luke took the flashlight Neoma extended to him. He was clearly turning a deaf ear to her pleadings. "Open up," he instructed.

She popped her mouth open in a wide and exaggerated pose. He grasped her chin between his fingers to inspect her throat. Their eyes met briefly.

"It's just a himple caze of tonsihites," she garbled as he held her mouth firmly open.

"Could be," he murmured distractedly as he pointed the rays of light down her throat. "But then tonciletiemosis has the same symptoms."

She frowned. "Whut's tonciletiemosis?"

If he thought trying to carry on a conversation with your mouth propped open like a jack-in-the-box was easy, he was nuts!

Luke lifted a disbelieving brow. "You've never heard of tonciletiemosis?"

"Nooob . . . whut ees hit?" Her eyes broaded farther.

"A rare, debilitating disease that . . . oh surely you've heard of it." He was acting as if she was kidding him.

"I'b neber heard ob suzh a diseese!" she scoffed, but her pulse did give a queer little leap at the mere thought of such a malady.

"You're serious? Well," he said in a grim tone, "the voice goes first, then the eyes . . . then the mouth. . . . Well, let's just say it's a heck of a way to go."

Her eyes widened more fearfully as he finished his examination and tapped her now gaping mouth shut.

"Well?" she prompted.

"Well, what?"

"Do I have tonsillitis?" She knew he was only trying to scare her with all that foolish talk about toncile-tiemosis, but yet with Luke you never knew. . . .

"It's entirely possible."

"Possible! Of course I have tonsillitis! Any fool can see that!"

Luke was unperturbed by her self-diagnosis as he turned his attention back to Neoma. "Or she could have strep throat. There's no way of knowing until they get some cultures on that throat."

"That's what I thought!" Neoma exclaimed triumphantly.

Cassie groaned with exasperation as a new round of chills assaulted her.

"Well, that settles it. Uriah will just have to take her back to Macon when he gets home this evenin'," her mother announced.

"Probably be a good idea." Luke nodded. "Well, guess I'll be running along. Oh, by the way, Cass, I don't think it is tonciletiemosis, but you can never be too careful. If your temperature goes up another notch, and you feel the skin around your neck and facial muscles begin to sag. . . ." He shook his head pensively. "Of course, I'm not a 'people doctor,' but I'd still strongly advise you consult another doctor real quick."

When Neoma left to see him out Cassie was still peeping up over the blankets looking considerably more concerned than she had been a few moments earlier.

"She'll be all right," Luke comforted a few moments later when they were out of Cassie's hearing range. "It's her tonsils all right, but it would be wise to get a culture taken."

"Yes, that's what we'll do, but I have no idea what time Uriah will be back. Sometimes those Grange meetings last till midnight."

"Well"—they paused as they reached the kitchen and his fingers toyed with his large Stetson—"you know I'd be more than happy to take her, but she wouldn't hear of it."

"You would?" Neoma's face brightened at his suggestion. "Now let's not be too hasty. She just might change her mind and decide it's best for her to go."

Luke shook his head negatively. "Not a chance. Not with me, at least."

Neoma smiled deviously. "If you're serious about taking her, you wait right here."

Luke shrugged and pulled out a chair from the kitchen table. "Don't get your hopes up," he warned as he pitched the hat on the table and made himself comfortable. "I guarantee you, she won't go."

"Wylie, you fix Luke something cold to drink," Neoma ordered as her youngest son walked into the kitchen looking for a snack. "I'll be right back."

Ten minutes later Luke was finishing his glass of tea when to his surprise Neoma and Cassie walked into the room.

He shot to his feet, hardly able to believe his eyes. Cassie was wearing a heavy sweater and carrying her purse, but the scowl on her face assured him she wasn't any too happy. She planted herself in the middle of the kitchen floor staring at him sullenly, but it was obvious she had consented to make the trip.

"Uh . . . you ready to go?" he asked cautiously.

"If I must."

Reaching for his hat, he motioned for her to precede him. "We'll take my car," she stated curtly. She didn't want to be indebted any more to him than was necessary.

"No, we won't," he said pleasantly. "We'll take my truck."

"Don't be an ass about this, Luke. I'm already imposing on your time. I don't intend to argue about this. We'll use my car and my gas."

"We'll take my truck and use my gas or we don't go," he stated flatly.

He wasn't about to drive her hot-shot car.

"For heaven's sake, Cassie. You can settle this later," Neoma intervened. "Now go get in the truck."

She looked at Luke sourly. If it wasn't for the fact that there was just the tiniest chance that she might have this . . . horrid tonciletiemosis thing, she would tell him what he could do with his truck and his far-fetched diagnosis!

"Are you coming or not?" he challenged.

"I'm coming, I'm coming," she muttered, but the look she gave him made it plain she was doing so under duress. She swept around him haughtily and headed for his truck.

"I really appreciate what you're doing," Neoma told Luke as he prepared to follow.

"It's all right, Neoma. I'm glad to do it for you."

"Cassie—well, she don't mean to be so spiteful,"

Neoma apologized. "She's just a little stubborn at times."

Luke's gaze followed the young woman, who was carefully making her way out to his vehicle. "Yes, I've noticed that." He'd like to turn that fancy little tail end of hers over his knee and give her a sound paddling, and he just might if she kept defying him. "How did you ever talk her into letting me take her to the hospital?"

"Oh," Neoma sighed, "I just told her I knew someone who had died of that tonciletiemosis thing, and she shouldn't be taking any chances."

Luke's grin was definitely guilty now as he dropped his eyes in repentance. "Aw, Neoma. I was only teasing her about tonciletiemosis. There isn't any such disease. I only made that up to get under her skin."

"Oh, I know that!" Neoma grinned. "But it worked like a charm, didn't it?"

"Yes, I guess it did." He sighed and stuck his hat back on his head. "Well, this ought to be interesting."

"She'll be fine once you're on the road," Neoma predicted.

Cassie was still slowly gaining on the truck when Luke stepped out the door and hurriedly caught up with her. The fever was making her light-headed and she suddenly found herself very unsteady on her feet. Before she knew what was happening he had picked her up in his arms and was carrying her the rest of the way.

"Will you put me down!" she protested indignantly.

"You're staggering around like a Saturday-night drunk," he observed calmly.

"I am perfectly capable of taking care of myself!"

"Maybe so, but right now I'm taking care of you, so you might as well pipe down." He reached the truck and shifted her to his knee unceremoniously as he opened the door.

Moments later she was meticulously being tucked in the front seat and the door was being slammed with the authority of someone who was confident he had the final word.

Or so he thought.

CHAPTER FIVE

"I still say we should have taken my car," Cassie continued to grumble thirty minutes later as they bumped along the highway to Macon in Luke's truck. The Jag rode like a dream while this truck rode like a lumber wagon, and she didn't hesitate to tell him so.

"Well, Her Majesty will just have to put up with the inconvenience," Luke retorted. "If I'm taking you, you're riding in my vehicle."

"Look at your gas gauge," she complained. "You're running on fumes, you know."

"I have plenty of gas," he argued.

"Does your E on your gauge stand for something different than the E on my gauge?" she persisted.

"I don't know. What does your E stand for?" For someone who supposedly felt bad, she sure could be a pain in the butt.

"Empty."

"Well mine means almost empty. That's what you get for buying those high-priced pieces of junk. My truck will run another twenty miles once it reaches the E," he said smugly.

She ignored his tacky reference to her Jaguar. He was only jealous and she knew it. "Why, oh why, did this have to happen now?" she lamented woefully. It suddenly seemed as if the whole world was against her. "I'm leaving for New York day after tomorrow and I'm going to feel awful for the drive home!"

"Stop feeling so sorry for yourself," he complained. "Maybe you'll leave, and maybe you won't."

"Now what's that supposed to mean?"

"It means you may go back to New York and then again you may not," he repeated. "That throat looks pretty bad to me and, personally, I don't think you'll be going anywhere in the next couple of days."

"Don't bet on it. I'll get back to New York if I have to crawl."

Luke glanced over at her impatiently. "You really hate it here, don't you?"

"Yes." The rapid, sharp affirmation hurt her throat. "I mean no, I don't hate it here," she added softly, trying to temper her harsh words. "I always enjoy being with my family and I love seeing old friends, but I can't deny I'll be happy to get back home."

"This is your home," he returned quietly.

"Not anymore." Even as she said the words she felt a terrible feeling of disloyalty to all those who loved her and were so terribly proud of her.

"That's too bad. I found that all the years I was gone I missed the town very badly," he confessed.

It would have been much easier on her guilt if he had picked this time to be his usual, arrogant self.

A humble Luke Travers was frustrating.

"Are you warm enough?" He reached over and tucked the sweater around her closer, changing the subject for the moment.

A nice Luke Travers was even harder to take.

"Yes, thank you."

"It's not much farther now," he noted as he eyed her feverish glow in the lights of the dashboard. "Can I do anything for you?" He had to admit she looked pretty miserable.

"No, I'm fine . . . really." She hugged the warmth of the wool around her tighter, trying to still another round of chills. "Just ge-t me to th-e hospital s-o I can get some re-l-ie-f."

"Neoma said Uriah had to go to Macon tonight," Luke said conversationally as he tried to adjust his side vent for a better flow of air. The temperature was extremely uncomfortable, but since Cassie was having chills he had left the air conditioner off and rolled down his window.

"Ye-s, he-'s at some mee-t-ing."

"He going to have to learn to take it a little easier," Luke pondered. "His blood pressure has been acting up lately."

"He's always had high blood pressure," Cassie pointed out. "Are you hot?" She noticed he was perspiring heavily and periodically mopping at his brow.

"A little." He smiled at her and shook his head. "Looks to me like you'd be burning up in that sweater."

"I wish I had two more," she confessed, and huddled deeper into the warmth. "Why should Dad take it easier? He's always enjoyed wor-k-ing hard." She returned to their earlier conversation, puzzled as to why her father's health kept popping up. First Rosalee, then her mother's vague reference, and now Luke had mentioned he was worried about him.

"I know he has, but he's not a young man anymore,

and I think he's been pushing himself too hard lately. Were you aware he stayed up with that calf again all last night?"

She hadn't known that. For a week and a half the calf had clung precariously to life, and for most of that time Uriah had been at its side. "Well, he shouldn't be doing that," she agreed. "But he's used to working hard."

"Maybe so, but he doesn't seem himself lately."

"Is the calf going to make it or not?" It seemed to Cassie that was what was putting all of the pressure on her father at the moment. He had babied the calf like he would one of his own children had they been ill.

"She's a little scrapper, but I don't see how she's held on this long. The calf has a rare disease that's almost always fatal, and I think it's only a matter of time before it dies."

"Then Dad will lose it?" For some reason the calf had taken on a special meaning for Uriah and she knew its death would hurt her father deeply, especially after he and Luke had fought so long and so hard for its life.

"I could be wrong, but yes, I think we'll lose it," he confirmed softly.

Her gaze fell back uneasily on his gas gauge. The needle wasn't even rocking now. "Luke . . . don't you think you should try to find a gas station?" He was making her extremely nervous. She never let her tank get that close to being empty.

"No, I have plenty of gas."

The lights of the hospital loomed in the far distance as Luke flipped on his turn signal, then shot off the exit ramp. "Besides, we're almost there now. I'm going

to take the access road and we'll make better time
. . ." As he spoke the truck sputtered a couple of
times, then began to jerk along erratically.

Cassie glanced over at him worriedly. "What's
that?"

"What's what?" he asked innocently as he began to
pump the gas pedal rapidly.

"That noise."

"I don't hear anything."

By now she didn't either. The engine had belched
one final time and then stopped altogether. They rolled
along another quarter of a mile before the truck glided
to a complete halt.

She slowly turned her head to face him. "Well"—
she drummed her fingers impatiently on the seat—
"what now?"

He grinned sheepishly. "I'll check under the hood.
It acted like the fuel pump."

"No, it's not the fuel pump," she stated calmly.
"You're out of gas."

"No, I'm not out of gas," he denied again. He jerked
the door open and got out.

"You are too!" she exploded. "I had a perfectly
good car sitting there with a full tank of gas, but we
had to take your truck. Didn't I tell you ten minutes
ago you were running low on—" Her words were sev-
ered as he slammed the door shut and stalked around
to the front of the truck.

Stubborn! Stubborn man! He was out of gas! She
seethed.

After tinkering unsuccessfully under the hood for a
few minutes, he returned to poke his head in the win-

dow once more. "It . . . uh . . . doesn't seem to be the fuel pump."

She patiently folded her hands in her lap in complete martyrdom. "Somehow, that doesn't surprise me at all."

He glanced around, trying to decide what to do. "I guess I'm going to have to call a wrecker."

"Where?" As far as she could tell, there wasn't a place between here and the hospital where he could use a telephone.

Luke's gaze fell in the direction of the hospital, then back at her sheepishly. "Looks like the hospital's about the closest. Think you can make it?"

Her head shot up. "You mean . . . walk?"

"Well, yeah . . . or I could go make the call, then send a cab back for you," he offered.

Cassie tried to judge just how far the hospital was from where they sat. It couldn't have been more than a mile or so, yet the thought of walking there when she felt so bad was not the least bit appealing.

"Maybe another car will come along and give us a ride," she pleaded.

"That's possible, but it's getting pretty late and this road isn't traveled all that much."

With a low groan, she grabbed the handle and pushed the truck door open. She supposed she had no other choice but to walk, but the thought irked her. Especially when she knew she would have been there by now if they had only taken her car.

"Oh, this is appalling. I have to walk to the hospital when I'm sick and it's freezing cold—"

"Just stop your squawking. You'll live, but I may not." He was there to lift her down onto the ground, then carefully button up the heavy sweater so she wouldn't get chilled again. She grumbled and muttered and blustered irritably under her breath, but she complied patiently as his large fingers ran into trouble securing the tiny pearl fasteners.

"Why don't they just put zippers on these things?" he complained.

"They wouldn't be as pretty."

"But they'd work better."

"Hurry, I'm freezing again." She shivered radically.

"Lord, Cass. It has to be a hundred out here!" he groaned. His face was beet red and as flushed with heat as hers was.

It was several moments before he finally completed the task of buttoning her sweater, and by now perspiration was rolling in streams down the sides of his face. "There. You shouldn't get cold now," he said with the complete confidence of a man who was standing at the gateway of hell.

He reached up to remove his hat and run his shirt sleeve over his brow. It was obvious he was sweltering.

"I'm still a little chilly," she confessed meekly.

He sighed and shifted his weight to one foot, a habit she was beginning to recognize when he was trying to be agreeable. "You want my hat?" He didn't have anything else to offer her in the line of warmth.

She nodded gratefully. It was crazy, but even her ears felt cold.

The hat was ridiculously large on her, but by now she was past caring about fashion. "How do you think you're going to see?" he chided as he tried to adjust the hat so that she would still have partial vision.

"It's fine. You wouldn't happen to have any gloves . . . would you?"

"Gloves?" He looked at her blankly. "We're just going about a mile down the road."

"But my hands are like icicles," she objected.

Gloves . . . gloves . . . ? He thought for a moment, and then began to rummage around under the seat of his truck and jubilantly came up with a ragged, crumpled-up pair a few moments later.

"They're not much to look at, but they'll keep you warm," he told her as he helped her slip them on. He stepped back to survey her and the sweat beaded anew on his forehead. "Surely you're warm enough now?"

She peeked back at him from beneath the wide brim of his hat and grinned. "I think so."

"Good, I'm about to have a heat stroke," he confessed with an audible sigh of relief. He absently tucked an errant strand of her dark hair beneath the hat.

"Hey, look. Why don't you cheer up? You don't have that many problems. God's still in his heaven, we've finally got you warm enough, the hospital is just a ten-minute walk from here, Doc Lydell will give you an antibiotic, and in no time at all you'll be on your way back to New York."

She gave him a wavering smile. Maybe he was right. Maybe it wasn't so bad after all.

"As far as I can see, you've got only one problem."

"What?"

"You forgot to put your dress on."

Her gaze flew down to her sweater and it belatedly occurred to her that during all the rush she had completely forgotten to get dressed!

"Oh, for heaven's sake! Why didn't you say something sooner!"

He shrugged and reached into his pocket for a smoke. "I was thinkin' about it, but I didn't know how to bring up the subject without embarrassing you."

Gathering the sweater around her throat tightly, she scowled at him menacingly. "Well, you could have at least given me a clue!"

They started off down the road and Cassie prayed no one she knew would see her. Even in New York anyone walking down the highway at night, with the temperature hovering around eighty-five, wearing a slip, a sweater, gloves, and a gigantic cowboy hat, would look a little odd.

"I'm sorry about this," Luke apologized as they walked along.

"You should be. If we had taken my car—"

"I said I was sorry," he stated again sharply.

"You just didn't want to ride in my car," she accused, feeling decidedly out of sorts with the whole world. He wouldn't let her take the Jag and now she was wandering around half dressed, like some pervert! For some strange reason she and Luke had always been competitive with each other. It was silly, but nevertheless it was true, and now that she had become highly successful in her field and could afford a nice luxury car, he was going to try and ignore it.

Taking her car to the hospital would have meant an admission on his part that she was doing just as well as he was. But it was clear he wasn't about to do that. He just couldn't stand it that Cass McCason was driving a Jaguar and he was still driving a pickup!

"That's ridiculous. Why should I mind riding in your car?" he asked indifferently.

"Because it is my car."

"And you think that worries me?" he asked incredulously.

"Doesn't it?"

"If all I had to worry about was what kind of car you drove, I'd give up!" he informed her irritably.

Cassie didn't have the strength to continue the argument. Luke noticed her weakness, and he put his arm around her and half carried her into the hospital. They didn't speak because it was clear that Cassie was too sick to talk.

As far as Cassie was concerned, she just wanted to get this miserable night over and start back to New York the day after tomorrow.

As far as Luke was concerned, day after tomorrow couldn't come fast enough.

When they reached the hospital there were a few inquisitive stares as Luke held the emergency-room door open and let her enter. The nurse who was sitting at the desk glanced up as Cassie marched up and asked for Dr. Lydell to be paged.

While they took her to an examining room Luke went in search of a telephone. She immediately stripped out of her bizarre wardrobe and asked the nurse for a blanket to wrap around her. It was twenty minutes before the doctor arrived to examine her, only to confirm what she already knew.

She had another raging case of tonsillitis.

"Those things are going to have to come out one of these days," he warned as he tossed the tongue depressor into the wastebasket.

"I know. I just dread the thought."

"Nonetheless, they're not doing you any good. I want you to see your doctor and discuss the possibility of having them removed the minute you return to New York. In the meantime, I'll try to patch you up until you get back home."

"Thank you. I will," she promised, immensely relieved to know it wasn't that horrible tonciletiemosis thing.

He peered through his wire-rimmed glasses at her and winked playfully as his gruff tone softened. "See that you do, young lady, and no more excuses." He turned and gave the nurse some brief instructions, then turned back to her. "Was that Luke I saw out in the hall a few minutes ago?"

"Yes, Dad was at a meeting so he offered to bring me over here." She left out the part about having to walk the last mile because he had run out of gas.

"Hmm. Good boy. Good boy."

"Hmm," Cassie said, unimpressed.

"Guess he and Marilyn Hodges haven't gotten serious yet or I'd have surely heard," he speculated, more to himself than to anyone else.

"Marilyn who?" Cassie's ears unwillingly perked up at the mention of Luke's private life.

"Marilyn Hodges. Oh, yes, I suppose you wouldn't know her. She opened up an interior decorating shop here in Macon about a couple of years ago. Lovely girl, just lovely," he praised.

"And Luke's going with her?" Strange that made her stomach feel a little fluttery all of a sudden.

"Oh, they're seen together occasionally," Doc chuckled. "The whole town's sort of been hopin' something will come out of it. It's high time he took a wife and settled down." He sighed—almost romantically. "They make such a nice-lookin' couple."

The image of the small blonde dancing in Luke's arms the night of the party stampeded her mind like a herd of buffalo. They were a nice-looking couple. And Marilyn had gazed into Luke's eyes like a lovesick calf. . . . Cassie shook the disturbing image away. "Luke hasn't mentioned her to me."

"No, I suppose not," he mused, then chuckled knowingly. "Well, it's good to see you again," he said pleasantly as he sat down at a small desk and reached for a prescription pad. "It's been a while since you've been home."

"Yes, I'm afraid it has been."

"Staying very long?" he inquired as he began to write on the pad.

"No, my two weeks are nearly over. I go back home day after tomorrow."

"Oh? Well"—he ripped the piece of paper off and handed it to her—"that's too bad. I know Uriah and Neoma love havin' you." His face suddenly turned a bit more somber. "By the way, how is your dad?"

"He's fine."

"Good. Good. I'm glad to hear he's been takin' care of himself. I warned him a couple of months ago he needed to slow down." He pointed to the prescription he had just given her. "You can have that filled at the pharmacy here in the hospital before you go."

"Thanks. I will." She safely tucked the piece of paper into her purse. "It was good to see you again."

"Good to see you again, Cass. Take care of yourself." He left the room as Cassie was hurriedly crawling back into her sweater.

The nurse had informed her that Luke was taking care of the truck while the doctor completed his examination. He had left word he would be at the front of the emergency exit when she was ready to leave.

By the time she had the prescription filled he was waiting for her.

"What did the doctor say?" he asked as she got into the truck and shut the door.

"Tonciletiemosis my foot! He said I had plain old tonsillitis." She plopped his hat back onto his head forcefully. "Just like I thought."

"Lucked out, huh?" He readjusted the hat, then glanced in the rearview mirror before he put the truck into gear, then pulled out onto the road. Cassie noticed the truck was running like a top and the gas gauge was registering full now, but she wasn't about to ask him how he accomplished that. It couldn't have been easy since there were only two gas stations in Macon and they both closed by 10 P.M. "Did he give you a prescription?"

She winced as she thought about the shot the doctor had given her, and where he had unceremoniously placed it. "Yes. He not only gave me a prescription, he gave me a shot too."

Luke chuckled. "And I don't suppose it was where you wanted it?"

"No, a little lower than I would have preferred," she verified.

And for the first time since she had known Luke Travers, he actually looked at her as if she were a woman and not some common housefly that continued to annoy him.

Strangely enough, his eyes had that unmistakable light of male appreciation as his gaze slid casually over her slender body in a most complimentary yet disturbing way. Moments later she could hardly believe it when he grinned at her and teased, "I always thought being a medical doctor would have more advantages than being a veterinarian."

She scowled disapprovingly at him, but she had to admit that for some crazy reason her pulse was suddenly beating faster. "Dr. Lydell asked about you," she said sweetly.

"Oh?"

"Yes. He wanted to know if you and Marilyn were serious yet," she said innocently.

"Oh?" He reached into his pocket and withdrew a cheroot and stuck it in his mouth as he punched in the lighter on the dash.

"Yes, that's what he asked." She watched him light the cigar in silence; all of a sudden he had chosen to remain infuriatingly evasive. "I told him I didn't know," she added, hoping to keep the subject alive a little longer, although she had no idea why.

He looked over at her through a cloud of smoke he had just exhaled. "That would be a tough one."

"Well, you're not . . . are you?"

"What?"

"Serious about Marilyn," she snapped. Good grief! You would think he had gone stone deaf!

His lids lowered in the sexiest manner and, again, her pulse did this funny little beat. "Now I can't believe that would be a question that would cause *you* to lose any sleep."

She cleared her throat nervously and felt herself blushing. She was thankful they were back out on the highway now and he couldn't see her as well in the dim lighting. "Well, of course I wasn't asking for my own information," she excused. "I just thought I should know if the subject ever came up again."

"Why in the world would the subject ever come up again?"

She shrugged lamely.

He turned his attention back to the road.

"Well?"

"Marilyn and I date each other occasionally."

"And?"

"We have a nice time together."

"That's it? You have a nice time together?"

"For the present, that's it," he verified calmly.

She was dying to ask him more about this mysterious woman, but she didn't dare. He would think she was asking because she was personally interested, which couldn't be farther from the truth.

"Do you feel better now?" he inquired a few minutes later.

"I wasn't upset because I thought you were serious about Marilyn!" she shot back defensively.

He shook his head in complete disgust. "I didn't mean that. I meant, are you still chilled."

This time she did blush. All the way to the roots of her hair. How could she have made a blunder like that? "Oh," she said meekly. "No . . . I'm fine . . . thank you."

"Let me know if you start again. I stopped and

picked up a heavier coat from a friend of mine in Macon in case you need it."

The completely unexpected gesture touched her heart and she had to admit that was very nice of him. "Thank you. I will."

They rode for another few moments in silence, then like a fool she blurted out, "I suppose Marilyn was the blonde on your arm at the party the other night?"

Once more he turned to level a stern, blue-eyed gaze in her direction, totally confused by now why she was suddenly so interested in Marilyn. "As I recall, I danced with several women that night, but Marilyn is blond and I did dance with her several times."

"So it must have been Marilyn," she concluded, trying to keep her voice light now.

"Why don't you try and get some sleep?" he suggested a little while later. "The shot is making you drowsy."

"I'm not the least bit sleepy," she argued, but on second thought she decided to take his suggestion.

She had made a big enough fool of herself in front of him for one day.

She snuggled down on her side and pretended to doze the rest of the way home.

But she was keenly aware that he sat next to her. In the dim interior of the cab, she wondered for the hundredth time how he could be the Luke Travers she used to know.

He was still as arrogant as ever, but somehow she sensed he could be tender with a woman if he wanted to be. A small smile curved her mouth as she thought about how he tried to button her sweater with his large fingers. He had been kind, almost tender, in his clumsy ministrations. And stopping by to borrow a heavy coat from a friend in this heat must have taken some nerve. She hoped it had been a male acquaintance. Her sleepy gaze found the coat lying between them on the seat and she breathed a sigh of relief. It was a man's garment.

Yes, she bet he could be extremely gentle with a woman when he made love to her. . . .

He was concentrating on the road, deep in thought now. He was probably thinking about Marilyn. Marilyn with her blond hair and blue eyes and knockout figure.

She drowsily tried to focus on his profile as she grew warm and sleepy. Ruggedly handsome, virile, masculine, strong chin, just the right size nose, long, beautiful lashes, blue—incredibly blue—eyes . . . and he had a dimple in his left cheek when he smiled. . . .

Things became increasingly hazy after that. She was vaguely aware of the truck ceasing its rocking motion. Then she was lifted into a set of incredibly strong arms and carried into the house.

She remembered murmuring a soft protest that she was able to walk, yet her arms clung tightly around a warm neck that smelled faintly of soap and a musky after-shave.

The chest she was pressed tightly against was broad and comforting, and whoever was carrying her did so with the greatest of ease and gentleness.

Somewhere, far, far away, she could hear her mother thanking Luke for taking her to the hospital, then her shoes were being slipped off and she was being slid between cool sheets that smelled like they had been dried outdoors in the fresh sunshine.

Then Neoma was saying good night to Luke and he was saying good night to Neoma. . . .

She was aware her throat didn't hurt nearly as much as it had and she sighed softly as she snuggled down deep within the cocoon of the blankets that had carefully been tucked around her.

The faint click of the lamp beside her bed being turned off registered only briefly as the room was plunged into complete darkness.

Then something strange happened that caused her pulse to jump erratically in that funny way it had done twice already this evening.

Something warm and soft touched her forehead so very lightly she barely felt it. Then that delicious, gentle warmness touched her eyes, then her nose, then traveled down slowly until it touched her mouth.

It lingered only briefly, as if it somehow knew it was partaking of forbidden yet completely irresistible fruit.

She thought the warmness tasted musky . . . and sweet, and it made her think of Luke.

She tried to will her eyes back open so that she might draw that wonderful feeling back down to her, to sample and explore that sweetness, but the darkness that held her so tightly increased its hold until it completely overpowered her.

Tomorrow she would think about how nice it was, she promised herself as she dropped deeper and deeper into the strange black void that totally encompassed her now, or even more important, what it was. . . .

CHAPTER SIX

The heat of his kisses seared a molten path down the long, silken column of her neck.

"No, darling. It's wrong. We cannot allow ourselves to give in to this madness," she cried out.

"Wrong? Wrong? How can you say it's wrong when you know it's what we both want," he argued with a tortured groan.

He kissed her again passionately, his tongue swirling hotly in her mouth, and she hated herself, but she felt her defenses weakening.

"But Carolyn . . . we must think of Carolyn," she pleaded, knowing that within moments she would cast all sanity aside and let him make love to her . . . even as his wife, and her best friend, lay dying in the hospital after a crazed psychopath had tampered with the anesthetic in a simple operation to remove a plantar's wart from her left foot.

How could she do this to Carolyn, who had been like a sister to her?

She could only plead love. From the moment she had met Dr. Josh Mitchell she knew this hour was inevitable. He was like a jungle animal and she his powerless prey. . . .

The screen door banged shut as Wylie entered the living room, abruptly interrupting the soap opera Cassie was deeply submerged in lying on the sofa.

By the condition of his dusty face and even dirtier baseball suit, she could only guess that if his team hadn't won, then he had at least played hard that afternoon.

"Hi, how did it go?"

"Okay."

"Did you win?"

"No, but it was close." He disappeared into the kitchen and came back a few minutes later with a handful of cookies and a tall glass of milk.

Cassie glanced up from the screen and smiled as he plopped down in a chair across from her and began hungrily to gobble down the snack. "What was the score?"

"Twenty-six to five."

Her mouth dropped open. "And you consider that close?"

"Yeah," he returned between gulps of milk. "We got beat thirty-five to nothin' last week."

She laughed at his enviable optimism and turned her attention back to the television. Since watching soap operas was a rarity to her, she found herself fascinated with the complexity of the story line. If anyone ever thought they had a problem, this program would cure them of complaining forever. After watching what these poor people went through day after day, one would have surmised their everyday problems were minor in comparison.

"You feelin' better?"

"Yes, I think I am." Between the medicine and the

shot the doctor had given her last night, she thought she could feel a small improvement in her throat today.

"You still going home tomorrow?"

"Yes, I still plan to." She grinned at him impishly. "Are you going to miss me?"

"Yeah." He quickly polished off the last oatmeal-raisin cookie in his hand and wiped his mouth clean with the sleeve of his shirt. He was a little embarrassed at her probing questions and he wished she'd stop putting him on the spot like that. But he guessed he shouldn't mind. She was pretty nice . . . for a sister.

"I'll miss you too. Maybe we can arrange for you to come and visit me in New York next summer," she tempted. "I could take you to see the Statue of Liberty and the United Nations building. We can go for a ride through Central Park or take a sight-seeing boat around Manhattan Island. I know this neat little place that makes terrific hot-fudge sundaes we could go to afterward. Would you like that?"

"Yeah, that would be okay," he admitted. "But it would have to be after baseball season."

"Oh, sure. After baseball season," she agreed.

He looked around uncomfortably. "Where's Mom?"

"Down at the barn with Dad."

"Wonder what we're having for supper?"

"I think I might have heard fried chicken mentioned. You think that would do?"

Every member of the McCason family knew fried chicken was Wylie's favorite.

"Yeah. That would do." He grinned.

"And it seems to me I might have smelled a chocolate cake baking earlier."

Wylie's eyes grew rounder. "I hope she made it with fudge icing." He shot to his feet. "I think I'll go check."

While he was checking on the evening meal Cassie watched the remainder of the soap opera, experiencing a sharp pang of disappointment when she realized she wouldn't be able to see tomorrow's episode. She sincerely hoped that Eve and Josh were able to control themselves. Carolyn had enough trouble as it was.

The sound of the screen door slamming again captured her attention once more. She glanced up and saw her mother standing in the doorway, white-faced and shaken.

Cassie's blood immediately ran cold. She had seen that look on her mother's face only one other time in her life. The night Pauly had been involved in a bad tractor accident and it had been hours before they knew if he would live or die.

"Mom?" Cassie cautiously lifted her head from the pillow. "What's wrong?"

"Get Doc Lydell on the phone."

"What's wrong?" Cassie asked again blankly.

"Just get the doctor, Cassie. Quickly!"

"Dad . . . is it Dad?" She knew she should be making some sort of move to do as her mother had instructed, but some strange paralysis was keeping her imprisoned on the sofa.

A strangled sob escaped her mother as she moved across the floor and grabbed for the telephone. "Go down to the barn with your daddy, Cassie. Stay with him until I can get help."

Springing off the sofa, Cassie barely heard her mother dialing the phone as she slipped her shoes on with trembling fingers, then raced out the front door. Wylie had heard the commotion and followed on her heels out the doorway. They ran toward the barn as Cass's heart pounded in her throat. She didn't have the least idea what she would find when she got there.

What she found when she opened the door was her big, strong father, a man who had never stayed in bed a day of his life, lying on the floor beside the small calf. His eyes were closed and his face was pasty white, and Cassie's heart nearly stopped as her steps faltered in uncertainty.

Was he still breathing?

She had no way of telling, but he was lying so still and lifeless it made her grow weak with fear.

The calf lifted a wobbly head to stare at the new intruder, and then with a pitiful sound it fell weakly back down on the soft pile of hay someone had lovingly placed it on.

Hesitantly, she reached out to touch her father's shoulder. "Pop?"

Instead of the familiar, booming voice she would have once heard in response to her call, there was only the eerie sound of the wind whispering through the walls that echoed back to her.

The heat in the old barn was blistering, and combined with her nerves and recent state of health, she felt her body begin to weave with dizziness.

"Pop," she pleaded, willing him to open his eyes and look at her. But his eyes remained closed as her trembling fingers began to search for a pulse. It was several moments before she was able to locate one, but with a cry of relief she finally felt the sign of life she had been searching for at the base of his throat. It seemed very weak, but it was definitely there.

Tears were running down her cheeks now as she buried her face in her hands and wept with gratitude. He was still alive!

"Is he dead?" The sound of Wylie's shaken voice brought her momentarily back to her senses. He was staring at his father, his face an ashen gray.

"No . . . no. He's still breathing." She drew his small frame into her arms and she felt his body trembling nearly as hard as hers was.

A shaft of sunlight spread across the floor of the barn as she heard the door open once more. She raised tear-laden eyes to see Luke step into the barn, his eyes quickly assessing the scene before him.

With cool efficiency, he strode over to Uriah and knelt down. Within moments he had made a hurried examination of the older man and glanced back over at Cassie. "It's okay. He's still alive."

She nodded mutely, for once immensely thankful for his presence. "Were you here . . . ?"

"No, Neoma just called."

She glanced back to Uriah. "Is it his heart?"

Luke shook his head negatively. "I think he's had a stroke. Get me that old blanket over in the corner."

"But it's so hot. . . ."

"Do as I say, Cass," he instructed softly.

In a daze, Cassie did as she was told and seconds later Luke was making her father as comfortable as possible. "Neoma called an ambulance. It should be here in a few minutes." Luke began to speak to Uriah in loud tones, trying to elicit some sort of response.

"Mom . . . she should be here with him. . . ."

"She's still trying to locate Doc Lydell." As he spoke Neoma rushed into the barn and rushed back to her husband's side.

"Is he . . . ?"

Luke shook his head. "I haven't been able to get a response out of him, but he's hanging on, Neoma."

"Uriah . . . Uriah, please, dear God . . . answer me. . . ." Her voice broke off in a sob as she laid her head on the width of his broad chest and held him tightly. "Doc is going to meet us at the hospital, darling. . . . Hang on," she pleaded.

Luke stepped over and, in a gesture that made Cassie's heart wrench, took Wylie aside and talked to him for a few moments until she could see his trembling begin to subside. He spoke in soft, soothing tones, yet she knew he was helping the child to accept a situation that called for maturity far beyond his years.

When at last they heard the faint wail of a siren in the distance, Luke put a protective arm around the young boy's shoulders and they walked out of the barn together.

Only when her father had been placed in the ambulance and was on his way to the hospital did Cassie break down again. Neoma was riding with him, and as soon as Cassie informed the rest of the family what had happened, she would follow.

She was still in the barn, carefully folding the old, musty-smelling blanket, when Luke came looking for her.

It was a useless gesture.

The old blanket was worn out and dirty, but somehow by performing the simple everyday task it made the events of the last half hour more bearable.

"Are you ready to go?" Luke's deep voice barely intruded on her state of numbness.

"Yes . . . I need to call Pauly or Newt first. They can call Rosalee and Rowena and Rachel."

"I called Newt just a few minutes ago. He said they would meet us at the hospital."

Cassie felt a tremendous sense of relief that she wouldn't have to be the one to tell them. "Thank you, Luke."

She glanced up for the first time and saw him standing there in a shaft of sunlight. The rays made his hair look like spun gold, and the blue eyes that were usually alive with combativeness had lost a great deal of their sparkle now. It wasn't hard to see that his concern for her father was as great as hers.

"Thank you," she whispered again.

"Will you let me take you to the hospital, Cass?"

"Yes. I'd appreciate that."

She walked toward the doorway, and when she was even with him she looked up and started to thank him for helping Wylie earlier, but her eyes suddenly welled over with newfound tears.

He started to speak, but then changed his mind as his arms automatically opened to her and, without the slightest hesitation, she went into them.

Never had a man's chest felt so comforting or so welcome as the dam of emotion inside her completely spilled over.

He held her close as her racking sobs dampened the front of his shirt, and she wept out her fear to him.

"What . . . if . . . he . . . dies . . . ?" Death

95

was something she had never associated with her parents and she wasn't at all sure she could deal with such an unexpected turn of events.

"He'll have the best of care," Luke comforted. "We have a good hospital in Macon and Uriah's a strong man." He pried her gently away from his chest so he could see her as he spoke. "Try to look on the bright side. He's still alive, and that's something we can be thankful for."

"I know, but he looked so . . . so helpless." Her arms went around his middle and she buried her face back into his chest.

Her nearness, her vulnerability, her dependence on him at the moment made him almost heady. This was not the Cass he knew, not this warm, sweet-smelling, totally intoxicating woman. All of a sudden he found himself wondering what it would be like to fully taste the soft mouth that was always looking for a fight with him, or to look into her eyes and see desire and need instead of the usual defiance and rebellion that seemed to be there.

What would it be like to hold her body next to his, unfettered by clothing, unhampered by the sense of unspoken competition that always engulfed them? What would she do if he tried to kiss away her fears the way he longed to right now . . . ?

He pulled himself back to reality and silently chided himself for such inappropriate thoughts at a time like this.

With a reassuring pat, he gently lifted her away from him once more and smiled down at her encouragingly. "You better go do what all you women do to your faces before we go to the hospital," he prompted.

"Yes, I must look a mess," she hiccuped. "I'll only be a minute."

True to her word, five minutes later she was seated between him and Wylie and they were on their way to the hospital. For Wylie's sake they kept the conversation light and as normal as possible under the circumstances.

The entire family had gathered by the time they arrived. They were huddled in the small waiting room, apprehension and disbelief written on each face.

"I can't believe it," Rosalee cried. "He was fine this morning. Ray talked to him around nine and he didn't say a thing about feeling bad."

"Has anyone talked to Doc Lydell yet?" Cassie inquired expectantly.

"No, Mom came out a few minutes ago and said they were still running preliminary tests," Pauly said. "But it looks like a stroke."

It seemed longer than it actually was before they received any hopeful news. Late in the afternoon Dr. Lydell finally emerged to speak with the family.

"He's a lucky man," he began. "It was a stroke, but a relatively mild one."

There was an audible sigh of relief from the family.

"How is he now?" Cassie prompted.

"He's resting comfortably."

"Is Mom still with him?"

"Yes, I've allowed her to remain with him for the time being, but I want him kept extremely quiet for the next few days. Visitors will be limited," he warned. "Now why don't all of you go on home and get some rest yourselves? He'll be well taken care of and you'll be notified of any change if it becomes necessary."

"Don't you think someone should stay here with Mom," Rowena protested as the doctor disappeared back into the intensive care unit.

"I'll stay," Newt volunteered.

"And I'll relieve you," Pauly offered.

After considerable discussion concerning who would relieve whom, the family finally disbanded and went their separate ways.

Luke and Cassie decided to take Wylie to the coffee shop and feed him since it was now well past his dinnertime.

The hamburger tasted like cotton in Cassie's mouth, but she forced herself to keep up a cheerful demeanor for her brother's sake. He was taking Uriah's illness extremely hard. He barely touched his plate, choosing to spend most of the time questioning Luke about whether or not he thought his father would really be all right.

Before they left the hospital they stopped by the intensive care unit and spoke with Neoma for a few moments.

She looked drained and ten years older than she had when Cassie got up this morning, but there was a hopeful light shining in her eyes now.

"He spoke to me a while ago." She smiled. "He told me not to worry, he wasn't about to go anywhere without me." Her tears misted anew, then her brave facade crumbled as fast as it had manifested itself. "Ain't that just like him to joke about a thing like that? We've been together forty-seven years." She shook her head in wonderment. "Forty-seven years. Whatever in the world would I do without him?"

Cassie reached over to console her mother. "He'll be

fine, Mom. And he means what he says. He wouldn't think of going anywhere without you. You know that."

"Cassie, honey." Neoma took her hand. "What about you? Are you still planning on going back to New York in the morning?"

She hadn't thought about that. In the midst of all the confusion, leaving for New York had been the last thing on her mind. "No, I wouldn't dream of going back with Dad still in the hospital," she assured her.

"Well, I suppose it would be all right." Neoma tried to sound encouraging, but Cassie could still hear indecision in her voice. "Doc says Dad should be just fine. . . ."

"I know, and I'm sure he will be, but I'd just feel better if I stayed here until he gets out of the hospital."

"But what about your job?"

"I have a very understanding boss," she promised. "I'll stay and take care of Wylie while you nurse Pop back to health."

"Your sisters could do that, honey. We don't want to put any hardships on you."

"Mom, I wouldn't dream of doing anything else," she scolded gently. "Now stop worrying, okay?"

"You're a good girl, Cassie, and I appreciate your thoughtfulness. Doc Lydell said he could arrange a room for me here at the hospital so I can stay close to your dad. I don't expect I'll be home much in the next couple of weeks." She turned to bestow a big bear hug on her youngest son. "Now you behave yourself and mind what Cassie says, you hear?"

Wylie hung his head sadly. "I will."

"And see that you don't get behind with your chores."

"I won't."

"Luke." Neoma took his hand, her eyes shining with love for him too. "Take care of my children while I'm gone."

"I will, Neoma. You take care of Uriah."

"Oh, I will. I can promise you that."

The mood was lighter on the ride home, although Wylie seemed to be lost in a world of his own. In an effort to cheer him up, Luke stopped by the local Dairy Queen and bought them all chocolate cones, but Wylie ate only half of his. When they arrived back at the farm he went directly into the house without a word.

"You think he's all right?" Cassie asked Luke as she fell in step with him. He had told her earlier he needed to check the calf again before he went home.

"He'll be fine. It just sort of threw him for a loop. When you're nine years old you never think about losing one of your parents," Luke pointed out as he lit one of the cheroots he was fond of smoking.

"You don't think much about that when you're thirty," Cassie confessed.

"No, I suppose you wouldn't." The almost wistful way he said it reminded her that Luke had never experienced even having his own set of parents to be concerned about. Rumor had it that they had left him with his grandmother when he was barely old enough to crawl and just never returned to claim him.

"I guess you were too young to remember your parents?" As a rule, Cassie would never have pried into his personal life, but somehow the last few hours had drawn them closer to each other.

"The only thing I remember about them is the fact that they ran off and left me." The tone of his voice stated emphatically he was still very bitter about that. "That was a hell of a thing to do to a kid."

"But your grandmother loved you very much," Cassie said tenderly, trying to ease the pain she had unintentionally brought on.

"Yes, she did. She was a good woman, but it still wasn't like having a dad to play ball with or a mother who fixed pot roast every Sunday."

Once more she fought the urge to take him by the arm and make him stop walking long enough to tell him that it didn't matter.

They had reached the barn by now and suddenly Cassie felt apprehensive. The day had been hard enough on her emotions, and if the little calf that Uriah had fought so hard for had died while they had been at the hospital, she honestly didn't know if she could stand it.

"Luke." Her footsteps faltered and she paused.

"What?" He paused, too, and turned to look at her.

"I'm . . . I'm afraid."

"Afraid? Of what?"

"I'm afraid . . . the calf might have . . . you know."

In the soft rays of the moonlight she saw his tired features soften with realization of her newest fear and it suddenly occurred to her he must be near exhaustion. He had been out late the night before taking her to Macon, then back up bright and early this morning

101

to check on the calf before he went on with his other work.

"Yes, that's possible," he said carefully. He flipped the cigar out into the darkness and there was a shower of red sparks as it hit the ground.

"Do you think it . . . has?"

"I don't know, but if it has it's just one of those things that happens in life, Cass. We've worked very hard to save it, but if it wasn't meant to be, then it just wasn't meant to be."

"I know. It just doesn't seem right . . . not with Dad getting sick too."

"You're right. Life stinks at times." He smiled at her encouragingly. "So, you learn to hold your nose and go on."

She smiled at him timidly. "Maybe you'll have to teach me how."

"Simple." He reached out and pinched her nose together. "Just like that. Then tell the world to get off your back."

They both laughed delightedly.

"So, scaredy-cat, what do you think? Think we're brave enough to go take a look?"

She wasn't brave. Not in the least, but for some reason she didn't want him to have to go in there alone and face whatever lay beyond the door.

"Yes."

He started to push the door open and her hand reached up and stopped him. "Wait."

She was so near him now she could smell his after-shave, and her pulse gave a tiny flutter. She could never remember a time she was so acutely aware of a man. Her hand dropped away hesitantly, confused by these new feelings she was having toward him. "Okay, I think I'm ready now."

For a moment so brief that later Cassie would have to remind herself it did occur, their eyes met and held in the moonlight. They were so close it would have required little or no movement on his part to lean over and kiss her.

And, strangely enough, that was exactly what she wanted him to do.

His gaze ran over her moon-drenched features and he felt his breathing quicken, along with an unexpected ache growing inside of him. Lord, she was beautiful. Even after the day she had spent, she looked fresh and bright-eyed. Bright-eyed and bushy-tailed. That's how his grandmother would have stated it. How many men had there been in her life who had looked at her in the moonlight like this, then gone on to claim her lips the way he wanted to right now?

A soft breeze had kicked up and tossed her hair about her head appealingly. He didn't necessarily like the way she was wearing her hair nowadays. It was too chic for his taste, but he couldn't deny that it was still beautiful. He preferred the way she wore it in high school. She used to pull it back in a ponytail or just let if fall loose around her shoulders in a soft halo. He caught the faint scent of the floral shampoo she used and it brought to mind once more how she had allowed him to hold her in his arms earlier today. He would never have thought, not in a million years, he would ever have the privilege of holding her in his arms, however innocent it might have been.

"Luke?" Her voice snapped him out of his daydreaming and he quickly let his eyes drop away from hers.

"You ready?" he asked.

"Yes."

He pushed the door open and stepped inside. It was so quiet and so dark. She eased over closer to him.

"I don't hear any breathing," she whispered.

He took her hand supportively. "There's a light around here somewhere."

"Over by the grain bin," she instructed.

He started to edge in that direction and she moved with him. "I can get it," he offered.

"I think I'll come with you . . . if you don't mind." Her hand clasped his tighter.

They carefully made their way across the room in the darkness. "I hope no one's left a pitchfork lying around," Luke noted. The pain in his lower half was excruciating enough.

When they reached the wall where the light switch was located, he fumbled around and quickly found it. "You ready?"

She squeezed his hand harder and clamped her eyes tightly shut. "Go ahead."

Light flooded the old barn now as she heard Luke's surprised, "Well, I'll be . . . will you look at that!"

Her eyes popped open and she could hardly believe what she saw. Standing in the middle of the room on decidedly wobbly legs was the small calf, just looking at them.

"Wha . . . look at her! What's she doing?"

"Looking at us." Luke grinned.

The calf bellowed, not a good strong one, but a definite improvement over what she had been doing.

Luke walked over and knelt down beside it, his grin growing paternal. "Hey, little one. You had us worried there for a while."

The calf bellowed again, a little stronger this time as she nuzzled a shaky head in Luke's large hand. Luke glanced up at Cassie and his grin widened. "I think she might be hungry."

There was a great deal of scurrying around as they located a bottle and Cassie ran to the house to warm milk. With great joy they watched as the calf took the first substantial nourishment it had had in weeks.

Later, as they walked back to the house, Cassie was still on cloud nine. "She beat the odds, didn't she? She didn't have a chance and she came through with flying colors. Can you believe that! I can't wait to tell Dad."

Luke had to grin at her enthusiasm. There was once a time when Cassie wouldn't have taken any special interest in the outcome of a small, sick calf.

"Yes, she's a fighter, all right."

"You must love your work," she praised. "And you're so good at it!"

Praises for Luke Travers from Cassie McCason. What other wondrous miracles could this magical night possibly hold?

"Thanks, but the credit belongs to a higher source," he acknowledged. They had reached the back door now and she paused to say good night. "I don't think I'll be able to sleep at all," she sighed. "Too many things have happened today."

"Are you feeling better?" he asked.

"Gosh, I've been so busy I've forgotten all about me." She swallowed, then smiled at him. "I think I'll be fine."

"Well, take a hot bath and don't forget to take your medicine," he cautioned. "You're far from well, yet."

"Oh, Luke," she sighed again and gazed up at him, and once more he felt the wall of defense he had tried to build around himself crumbling. "That little calf has restored my faith in miracles."

He smiled down at her. "I'm glad."

"Against all odds. She did it against all odds. Doesn't that make you just want to shout?"

Actually, it made him want to kiss her, but he had to admit that would be against all odds, and it would probably take more than a mere miracle to tip the scales in his favor.

"Yeah, it's real nice," he said softly. "Real nice."

CHAPTER SEVEN

By the grace of God, Uriah's health began slowly to improve. Cassie's assumption that she had an understanding boss proved to be accurate. Rand Creble had told her to take as much time as she needed and return to work only after she was satisfied she was no longer needed in Rueter Flats.

Dr. Lydell was pleased with Uriah's recovery and predicted that he would be back home in no time at all.

Wylie seemed to be the only one who wasn't taking the illness in stride. The change of schedule had thrown him for a loop. He was used to large meals on the table three times a day, Neoma humming around the house while Uriah was tending the stock. Although Cassie tried to maintain the same homey atmosphere, it just wasn't the same.

She could see Wylie's confusion growing with each new day.

As bad as she hated to admit it, Luke had been the only stabilizing force during this crisis. Not only for Wylie, but in a strange sort of way he had made the days easier for her.

Her brothers came by to help feed the stock and to

assist in the general everyday running of the farm. Rosalee and Rowena and Rachel did what they could to help, but their own families demanded the majority of their time, so the burden of keeping affairs running smoothly still fell squarely on her shoulders. Running a farming household in Rueter Flats was a far cry from working in a large advertising firm in New York, but it seemed like any time a major crisis popped up Luke was somewhere nearby to prevent it from turning into a complete calamity.

But to be honest, things could have been worse.

There had even been days when she had found herself enjoying the simple pleasures of country life. She loved to wake up to the sounds of the birds chirping early in the morning and the way the old rooster crowed her awake long before she would normally be rising in New York. She developed a habit of taking her coffee and sitting out on the porch to watch the sunrise each new day. It was a beautiful, almost awesome sight the way that big old fiery orange ball came sliding slowly out of the eastern sky. Although the day would usually be blistering hot, the early hours of the morning were delightful.

She was in the kitchen washing the breakfast dishes about a week after Uriah's stroke. Neoma had kept a constant vigil at his bedside, coming home only long enough to gather up clean clothing and see how things were going. Between daily telephone calls from Rosalee, Rowena, and Rachel, Cassie found it hard to keep up with all her chores. This morning she had been determined to get an earlier start than usual, before the telephone started ringing.

While she worked she had the radio playing and

several times she paused, aghast at times, to listen more closely to the commercials she was hearing.

True, she shouldn't be surprised at the amateurish, hickish way they went about advertising their local products, but still the creative side of her cringed when she heard such slogans as "Buy Grabe's Soap and Stop Your Mopes!" or the one advertising a new figure salon over in Macon that really sent her into fits: "Fatty Patty, Plump and Round, Join Slenderella for Just Pennies a Pound! Take That Fat Off Day by Day, Then the Men Will Start to Say, Hey!" Then they would go into a peppy little singing jingle giving the telephone and address of the new salon.

It would be amusing if it wasn't so pitiful.

If she had been a "Fatty Patty," she would die before she joined an establishment that called the whole town's attention to her problem.

What this area needed was a good advertising agency, she decided absently as she went about her dusting.

She glanced up a few minutes later as she heard a truck pull into the yard. Thinking that it was Pauly coming to feed the cattle, she went to the back door to meet him.

But it was Luke who got out and waved at her. She found herself smiling ear to ear and waving back at him. Darn, now she wished she had taken more time with her appearance this morning. She had showered and put on her regular attire of shorts and a T-shirt, but completely skipped the makeup routine.

"Hi! What's up?" she called.

"Pauly called and said one of the mares isn't acting right this morning. I'm going to check her," he called.

"Want some coffee first?"

"No, thanks. I'd love a cup but I can't spare the time."

"Oh, okay." She watched him walk to the barn, feeling a little let down that he couldn't visit for a while. Neoma had been right when she said he had changed. He had. A full 180-degree angle.

Actually, he was quite tolerable now.

She went back to her work but changed her mind a few moments later and went in and put on makeup, then dabbed a couple of drops of perfume behind her ear. A few minutes later she started out the back door with two cups of coffee in her hand.

Luke was in the barnyard with the mare, just completing his examination when she walked up.

"Hello there," she greeted again.

He glanced up, then quickly lowered his eyes back to the animal. Damn! Those shorts and that tight T-shirt shot his blood pressure up at least twenty degrees. "Hi."

"I thought since you didn't have time to come to the house, I'd bring your coffee out here." She smiled prettily and extended one of the cups to him. "Two teaspoons of sugar and a smidgen of cream. Right?"

"Right. Thanks." He stood up carefully, trying to ignore the way the T-shirt hugged her small breasts. But they weren't too small . . . actually just the right size . . . for him.

"What's the matter with it?"

"Nothing," he said absently, his gaze involuntarily going back to the tantalizing sight straining beneath the soft fabric. "They look great to me."

"Great? I thought it was acting strange."

He suddenly realized he was thinking about an entirely different subject. "Oh . . . the mare. Uh . . . I'm not sure yet."

She cocked her head and smiled at him puzzlingly. "What did you think I was talking about?"

"I'm sorry. I'm afraid my mind was wandering," he apologized, and she could have sworn he blushed, although it was hard to tell beneath his dark tan. He took a sip of his coffee, then grinned at her lamely.

"I have some coffee cake in the house if you're hungry," she tempted.

"Sorry, but I really can't today," he apologized again, then handed her back the cup. "I've got a couple of more calls to make, then I have to run out to the Pixley farm and pick up a piano for Reverend Copley."

"Oh, yes. Mom said Louella died and left her piano to the church."

"Yes. I told the Reverend I'd go pick it up for him today."

"Gosh, I wonder how Morgan's getting along by himself," Cassie mused. The Pixleys were an elderly couple who had no children and Louella had been the center of Morgan's life for nearly seventy years.

"I think he's pretty lonely." Luke had turned his attention back to the horse while they talked. "I try to stop by and visit with him a couple of times a week."

"That's awfully nice of you. I'll bet he appreciates the company."

"He seems to."

"I should make time to go by and visit with Morgan before I leave. Louella used to be my Sunday-school teacher," Cassie recalled fondly. "We used to have

111

wiener roasts and hayrides out at the Pixley farm when I was growing up."

Luke glanced up from his work. "I know. I was there at most of them."

"Oh, well sure you were," she said apologetically. How could she have forgotten? He used to torment her to death during those hayrides, stuffing hay down the back of her blouse and telling the most off-colored jokes he and his buddies could come up with behind the preacher's back.

She studied him more closely as he reached into his bag and prepared to give the horse an injection. That Luke Travers certainly grew up. Now he was a very thoughtful . . . incredibly fascinating man.

Why hadn't he married? If rumors were true, he could have had his pick of the available women he knew. An uncomfortable feeling stirred in her stomach at the thought of Marilyn. How serious was he about her? He had never mentioned her name except for the night she had brought up the subject on the way home from Macon.

Suddenly the memory of something warm and sweet touching her mouth that night after he brought her home from the hospital and carried her to her bed rushed back to her. Goose bumps welled up unexpectedly as she recalled the musky, exciting taste. The after-shave Luke wore smelled exactly like that memory had tasted. But it was ludicrous to think he would have kissed her.

For as long as they had known each other, up until the day Uriah had gotten sick, he had acted as if he couldn't tolerate her, let alone want to kiss her. Perhaps it was only the high fever she had that night that had made her imagination run away with her.

Her eyes played across the broad expanse of his back as he knelt down beside the animal and spoke to it in soothing tones. His shirt could not conceal the ripple of heavily corded muscles as he ran his hands consolingly over the mare, all the while talking to it as if it understood what he was trying to do. He was such a strong yet gentle man, and he spoke with such tenderness to the edgy mare that it quieted down immediately at his command.

What would Luke Travers be like when he made love to a woman? Would he still exhibit that same tenderness and sensitivity he was showing now or would his passion be as intense and as powerful as his magnificent body seemed to suggest?

The mere thought turned her knees to water.

"You doing anything special this afternoon?" she heard him ask while she was still thinking things she shouldn't be. It wouldn't do at all for her to suddenly find Luke attractive . . . in that sort of way. If they had been worlds apart as children, they were light-years apart now. She knew without even asking that he was content with his life here in Rueter Flats, while she on the other hand would never dream of leaving New York and moving back home. Yes, a romantic relationship between them would be highly improbable.

"Beg your pardon?" She hurriedly brought herself back to reality, even though her breathing had suddenly picked up its tempo.

Luke straightened up from his kneeling position and began to remove the rubber gloves he had put on earlier. "I asked if you were doing anything in particular this afternoon."

"No, nothing in particular. Why?"

He had been debating for the last five minutes whether or not to ask her if she would like to go with him to the Pixley farm, but he had finally come to the conclusion that all she could say was no, and he was fully prepared for that event. "I thought you might like to ride over to Morgan's with me when I go to pick up the piano." He turned back to the horse and shut his eyes, waiting for the refusal—or explosion, whichever came first.

She didn't have to be asked twice. "Yes, I'd like that."

"You would? Well, that's great." His shoulders went limp with relief. "I'll pick you up a little after noon," he offered, trying to keep the elation from spilling over in his voice.

"I'll be ready."

Around eleven Cassie found herself heading for the shower again. It was the second time this morning she had bathed, but she wanted to look nice for Morgan.

When Luke came to pick her up at noon, she looked prettier than a field of daisies. "You didn't need to dress up," he told her as he held the screen door open. The scent of her perfume drifted tantalizingly up to him as she ducked under his arm and walked out. But she had noticed he had showered and changed too.

"I didn't. I just thought a skirt and blouse would be cooler," she explained. The blue cotton peasant skirt and matching blouse were casual enough for any occasion. The blouse was worn off the shoulders and displayed enough creamy skin to quickly assure Luke that he was going to be perfectly miserable for the rest of the afternoon.

He helped her into his truck and then took his place behind the wheel. The cool air enveloped the cab as they drove out of the barnyard and headed north on the highway.

"What's Wylie up to today?"

"He's playing with the Edwards boy. They've been building some sort of a tree house all morning."

"Is he doing any better?"

Cassie sighed. "I don't know what's bothering him. He knows Dad is improving every day, yet he's been acting so strange."

"I've been meaning to take him fishing, but I've been tied up lately. I'll try to do it in the next few days."

"That would be nice."

Luke glanced over at her and grinned, the same devilish little grin he used to distress her with years before. "If you're a good girl, we might ask you to come along with us."

"I'm always good," she teased.

And he wouldn't have touched that line with a ten-foot pole.

The afternoon turned out to be one of the most pleasant Cass had spent in ages. Morgan was beside himself with joy when he learned he would have company for the afternoon. He made a huge pitcher of fresh lemonade and they sat their lawn chairs out under a large oak tree and patiently listened to him reminisce about his life with Louella.

At times his eyes would mist with unshed tears, then before they knew it he would be back to relaying some happy occurrence that would return a smile to his wrinkled old face.

The late afternoon shadows were growing lengthy across the lawn when Luke finally got up and folded his chair. "We hate to leave, Morgan, but Cass needs to be getting back home. Wylie will be wondering where she is."

The old man immediately got up also and folded his chair too. "I understand. I'll just call my neighbor to come help you load the piano."

Sawyer Middleton came driving up in his long black Cadillac twenty minutes after Morgan made the call.

Sawyer was in his fifties, pudgy, and always looked like someone had thrown him in a sack, shaken him up, then dumped him back out again.

"Luke, how are you, boy?" he greeted as he wallowed the big nasty-looking stogie he always smoked around in his mouth. Sawyer's family owned the majority of Rueter Flats, and their flamboyant life-style sometimes rubbed the citizens of the town the wrong way, but the Middletons were good about looking out for the best interests of their town.

Luke stepped over to shake Sawyer's beefy hand. "How's it going, Sawyer?"

"Fine as frog hairs." He beamed. His attention was instantly diverted to Cassie. "Lord almighty. Ain't you turned into a looker. The big city sure does look good on you, honey."

Cassie blushed at the blunt way Sawyer had of stating what he was thinking. "Why, thank you, Sawyer."

"Heard you're working in some big advertising agency up there in New York. Ya like it?"

"I love it," Cassie confessed.

"Hear you're doing right well too. Got yourself another big promotion, did you?"

"She sure did," Morgan chimed in. "We got us a right smart little gal here, Sawyer."

"Well, it's a pity she likes it so well up there," he sighed as he took his lighter out of his pocket and tried to reignite his cigar. Cassie studied the large diamond ring that was wedged tightly on his pinky. It must have cost him a mint. A huge puff of blue smoke boiled around his head as he continued, "When I heard you was back I kinda hoped you might be talked into opening up your own agency."

Cassie looked at him blankly. "In New York?"

"No, not in New York," he scoffed. "Right here in Rueter Flats."

"An advertising agency here in Rueter Flats!" Cassie burst into laughter. "Why, I wouldn't make enough money to buy corn flakes."

From the corner of her eye she saw a sudden, annoyed scowl cross Luke's face.

"Well, maybe not here in Rueter Flats," Sawyer retracted thoughtfully, "but Macon sure is big enough to accommodate such an agency. Why, folks around here have to go clear into Houston to get a good agency to represent them. Anything closer stinks."

Cassie would have to agree with him on that point. The local advertising she had heard on radio and television did indeed reek of inexperience.

"I think you're wasting your time, Sawyer," Luke stated quietly. "I don't think you could get her back to Rueter Flats with a whip and a chair."

Cassie shot him an offended look.

"Likes it that well up there, huh? Well"—he

shrugged his shoulders good-naturedly—"if you ever change your mind, Cass, let me know. I'll sure give you all of the Middletons' business."

Cassie's ears picked up. All of the Middletons' business. Mercy, that would practically support a small agency. And in a grand style too.

"Well, let's get this piano loaded." Sawyer grinned. "I got me a date with Estelle Mooney tonight." He wiggled his brows playfully at Luke and Morgan. "Oo-la-la. I'm tryin' to get her to marry me."

Cassie shook her head, laughing again. Sawyer had been married at least five times but he was apparently not at all discouraged by his deplorable record.

As Luke and the neighbor carried the old, upright piano out of the house and loaded it on the truck, Cassie saw Morgan quickly turn away and walk out behind the house to be alone.

She wanted to go to him and put her arms around him, to comfort him, but how would you comfort someone who had lost a part of themselves? The piano apparently represented just another part of Louella he was losing.

By the time they had it loaded, Morgan came back around the house to see them off. But Cassie noticed he never once looked in the back of the truck.

"Stop by and see me anytime you're in the neighborhood," he invited. "I've always got some fresh lemons on hand." His eyes unexpectedly misted again. "Louella always made sure we had lemons for folks that come by to see us."

Cassie reached over and hugged his neck lovingly. "I'll come and visit again before I leave."

"I'd like that," he said. "Tell Uriah I'm thinkin' about him."

"I will."

"It was real good seein' you again, Cass." Sawyer pulled out a large snowy handkerchief from his pocket and wiped at his heavily perspiring brow.

"It was nice to see you, Sawyer."

"Listen." He replaced the handkerchief in his pocket and leaned a little closer. "Don't dismiss that idea we were talkin' about earlier too quickly. You give it some thought. You hear?"

"I hear." She smiled.

Morgan turned and slowly made his way back into the house as Sawyer went to his car and Luke and Cassie got back into the truck.

"I'm not sure it's a good idea to let that piano ride like that. It might be wise to tie a rope around it."

Cassie leaned up in the seat and peered out the back window. "It looks like it's jammed in there pretty tight to me."

"It barely fit," Luke acknowledged.

"Then it should stay there without any trouble."

"I don't know. . . ." Luke eyed the situation carefully, then reached down and started the engine. "The thing probably weighs a ton. It should be all right. I'll take it easy."

They bumped along the gravel roads carefully and the old piano didn't budge an inch. When they reached the highway Luke felt confident enough to begin to pick up speed.

If the piano hadn't moved on the gravel roads, it sure wasn't going to move on the paved ones.

They were riding along, talking and thoroughly enjoying each other's company, and Luke was thinking more about the low cut of Cassie's blouse than he was the church's new piano.

By the time he went to make the sharp turn onto the highway leading home, they were fairly well flying low.

Luke was trying to light a cigar to take his mind off the scenery when the truck whizzed around the corner and all of a sudden there was the most horrifying clamor coming from the back of the truck. Sort of a Ping! Ping! Bong! Bong! Bong!

It sounded as if someone was trying to play the piano with a sledgehammer.

Frozen in their seats, Cassie cautiously turned her head to meet Luke's worried frown. Neither one of them had the nerve to look in the back of the truck.

"What was that?" she whispered.

"I don't know."

"It sounded like the piano fell out of the back of the truck," she said needlessly.

"It couldn't have!"

The truck slowed to a crawl and they both hazarded a glance at the bed of the pickup at the same time.

"It's gone," she announced grimly.

"Oh, hell."

"Luke." She was peering out the side of her window now, her hand clamped over her mouth in revulsion. "I think I see it. . . ."

He leaned over and his distraught eyes followed in the direction she was pointing. The piano was lying in pieces at the bottom of a culvert.

"Son of a . . . gun! What do we do now?"

"We'll have to pick up what's left of it and try to

explain what happened to Reverend Copley," she reasoned.

"How?"

"I don't know, but we can't leave it lying out there."

It took them well over an hour to gather up the remains of the piano. As Luke slid the last of the pieces into the truck he peered at her worriedly. "How are we ever going to tell him what happened?"

He could kick himself for not having his mind on his business. If he had watched the piano half as much as he had watched her gaping blouse, this would have never happened!

"The church will never get over this," he moaned. "Now I'll have to go out and buy them a new piano and I don't know a thing about buying pianos and—"

"Ooohhh. We'll just explain that it was an accident," she consoled as she stepped over to give him a reassuring hug. She could see he really felt bad about the loss and she didn't know anything else to do.

"I don't know, Cass. Everyone in the congregation was looking forward to having that piano," Luke fretted as his arms tightened around her possessively to return the embrace. "And what's Morgan going to say when he finds out what I did to Louella's piano?"

"He'll understand," she assured again, but she had been wondering the same thing.

She patted him on his back consolingly.

He patted her on her rear reassuringly.

"We'll tell him together," she promised. "It'll be just like getting up the nerve to go into the barn the night the little calf was so sick. You remember? Neither one of us had the nerve to go alone, but together we made it and everything turned out all right. And that's exactly how this will be."

But she felt considerably less brave as they pulled into the churchyard a half an hour later and Reverend Copley ran out to meet them with a grin the size of Texas on his face.

He peered anxiously into the back of the truck and the grin slowly began to fade as he viewed the mangled keyboard hanging out of the tailgate. "My word . . . what happened?"

Luke took a deep breath and pushed the truck door open reluctantly. "We better start looking for a new piano tomorrow," he whispered under his breath to Cassie. "But we'll make sure they deliver it."

As if the piano incident wasn't upsetting enough, when they arrived back at the McCason farm Wylie was nowhere to be found.

"I can't understand it," Cassie complained. "He hasn't touched the lunch I left, either."

"Maybe he's still over at the Edwards'," Luke suggested.

"He shouldn't be. I told him to be home by supper and it's way past that time." She picked up the phone and dialed the neighbor's number. Moments later she replaced the receiver, a frown forming on her face. "They said they can't find Davy, either."

Luke took off his hat and ran his fingers through his hair wearily. "They've probably lost all track of time. They'll be getting hungry before long."

"Do you think so?"

He replaced his hat and smiled at her. "I know so.

I'll go down and check the mare and I'll lay you odds he'll show up by the time I get back."

But Wylie had still not returned when Luke came back from the barn. By now it was growing dark and a dark cloud bank was moving in from the north.

"Luke, I'm worried. He's never stayed out this late before and it looks like a storm's coming up."

"Did you call the Edwards again?"

"Yes, and they're worried too. What shall we do?"

Luke sighed. "Let's go look for him."

"Do you have time?"

He glanced at his watch. "Can I use your phone?"

"Sure, go ahead." She walked over to the sink and made a pretense of getting a glass of water, wondering who he was going to call.

He didn't use the directory, but quickly dialed the set of digits by heart. "Hi," he said when the phone was answered on the other end. He leaned casually against the wall as he talked. "I'm afraid I'm not going to be able to make it tonight.

"No, I'm over at the McCason place. Wylie seems to have disappeared and I'm going to help Cass look for him."

Cassie would have given fifty dollars to know who he was talking to!

"Sounds good. Maybe tomorrow night.

"Yeah, I'll get in touch with you later." He placed the receiver back on the hook and glanced over at her. "You might as well ride over to my house with me. I have to pick up a few things, then we can leave from there."

"What if Wylie should show up here?"

"Leave him a note and tell him we're looking for him. Tell him to call my house as soon as he gets in."

Cassie hurriedly wrote the note and called the Edwards to inform them of her plans and asked if they had any suggestions where they should begin their search.

"Surely he's just lost all track of time." She tried to bolster her sagging spirits.

"I'm sure it's that or something equally simple," Luke agreed. He reached in his pocket for a cheroot.

"You smoke too much. It's bad for your health," she reminded.

"Don't start nagging me. I'm trying to be nice to you."

"I'm not nagging you. I'm only pointing out a well-known fact that smoking is harmful to your health."

"I know."

As they walked out the back door Cassie glanced over at him, her stomach doing that funny little flip-flop at his nearness.

"I hope this doesn't spoil your evening."

"It won't."

"The person on the phone didn't mind?"

"Didn't seem to." He struck a match and lit the cigar.

Oooooo! He could be so irritatingly tight-lipped at times.

"She wasn't upset?" Cassie tried a sneakier approach.

Luke paused, his blue eyes narrowing. "Did I say it was a she?"

"No . . . no. I just assumed . . ."

They started walking again.

"Then she didn't mind?"

"No, he didn't."

She was ashamed of herself, but she couldn't keep her face from brightening. "He . . . didn't?"

"That's right. He. I was supposed to have a beer with a couple of buddies tonight." He finally glanced down at her and she could see a faint smile tugging at the corners of his mouth now. "Okay?"

"Oh, okay." She shrugged indifferently. "I mean it doesn't really matter who it was, I just wanted to make sure I wasn't imposing upon your evening."

"Rest assured, you aren't."

She didn't know how "assured" she was by the whole matter, but she had to admit it did make her feel a lot better just knowing that he hadn't had a date with Marilyn.

CHAPTER EIGHT

The storm moved in while they were en route to Luke's house. He lived only a few miles down the road from the McCason farm, but by the time they had pulled into his drive the rain was pelting down on the windshield in big fat droplets.

"We'd better make a run for it," he warned.

They had barely reached the porch when the heavens opened up in a deluge and the wind and lightning began in earnest.

"I hope Wylie has taken cover," Cassie shouted above the wind.

"Give the kid a break, Cass. Of course he's taken cover. He's got a brain."

Luke opened the door and let her into the living room just as his phone started ringing. In three long strides he jerked up the receiver and barked, "Dr. Travers."

That was the first time Cassie had ever heard him refer to himself as a doctor and a thrill of pride shot through her.

"Yeah, Neoma." He shot Cassie a worried grimace.

"Is that Mom?" Cassie rushed over beside him.

"Don't tell her about Wylie yet. She'll only worry," she cautioned in a hushed whisper.

"Yeah, we've been looking for him."

Neoma said something and Luke's brow raised. "With you? How did he get over there?"

"Is he with her?" Cassie gasped.

"Wait a minute, Cassie's about to blow a fuse." Luke handed the phone to her and stepped back.

"Mom? Is Wylie there in Macon with you?"

"Yes, he and the Edwards boy decided to come and visit Uriah today. They hitched a ride in the back of a milk truck."

"Oh, good grief!" Cassie sank down on a chair and breathed a sigh of relief. "I bet you think I'm some baby-sitter to let that happen."

"I've already told him it was a foolish thing to do, but he seems to be taking his father's illness so hard, maybe it's best he spend a little time over here with him."

"I'll drive over and get him right now," Cassie promised.

"No, don't do that. It's getting late and I think it will do him good to spend some time with his daddy. I think he'll see that Uriah's really going to be fine and then he'll feel a whole lot better about the situation."

"But where will the boys sleep?"

"I'll make special arrangements with the hospital to let them sleep in my room tonight, then you can come over tomorrow and get them. Uriah wants to see you, anyway."

"Is he feeling better?"

"Much. The doctor thinks he'll be able to come home in another few days."

"Oh, that's wonderful . . . but, Mom, how did you know I was over here?"

"I called home first and when I didn't get an answer, I called the Edwards. They told me you and Luke were going to go out hunting for the boys so I thought to try his place."

"Well, I'm sorry I didn't watch Wylie closer." She went on to explain how she had spent her day and the disastrous incident with Louella Pixley's piano.

"Oh, how terrible," Neoma sympathized. "We needed that piano for our Sunday-school class."

"Luke's going to buy the church a brand-new one," she consoled. "Reverend Copley is elated."

When she hung up the phone it had been decided that she would drive to Macon early the next morning and retrieve the adventurous boys.

"Well at least he made it all right," Cassie said thankfully. She raised her eyes to meet Luke's and she suddenly felt uneasy. She had felt his gaze studying her as she had spoken with her mother and he was still staring at her with a strange light in his eyes, even now. She remembered the embrace they had shared earlier and she wondered if he was thinking about the same thing.

Granted, it had been at the intersection of a busy highway, with semitrucks and cars whizzing around them, but the impact was no less devastating than if they had been in a candlelit room with soft music.

Her gaze shyly dropped away from his and she gave a small nervous laugh as she smoothed her hand across her hair. "Well. All this trouble for nothing. As you said, he was perfectly all right." She hazarded a quick glance at him again. "If you hurry, you can take me back home and still keep your date to have that beer with your friends this evening," she offered.

"No," he said easily. "I'm bushed. I'll catch them another time. If you're not in any hurry, I'll just go and clean up."

"No, I'm not in any hurry," she agreed quickly. "With Wylie gone, I don't have a thing to do until tomorrow morning."

She had no idea why she was so relieved he hadn't taken her up on her suggestion to keep his date, but strangely she was.

"Make yourself at home. I won't be long."

While he was gone Cassie entertained herself by exploring the house. It was an old two-story farmhouse, but it had been well taken care of.

The downstairs had a large living area, a small den, a massive kitchen that was furnished with all modern appliances, and a large utility room with a commode and lavatory.

The living-room furniture was masculine, yet in extremely good taste. The room was decorated in shades of oatmeal and browns with splashes of navy blue throughout for accent. Two plaid love seats sat facing each other in front of a stone fireplace, with a massive round table made of glass sitting between them.

She surmised the bedrooms would be up the steep, carpeted staircase because she could hear the shower running somewhere overhead.

The den was all his. Comfortable mahogany and leather furniture, a beautiful oak desk, and rows upon rows of books in the shelves lining both walls told her this was the room Luke spent most of his time in. There was a small lamp burning on the desk, illuminating the pile of assorted papers he had strewn about. But otherwise the entire house was immaculate and orderly.

He came down the stairs while she was sitting on one of the love seats thumbing through a magazine.

He was still combing his hair as he entered the living room.

"My, that didn't take long," she complimented as she glanced up at him. The fresh smell of soap and after-shave drifted about enticingly and it made her slightly heady as she tried to focus her attention back on the article she had been reading.

Why was he affecting her this way? He was just a man, she reminded herself. A very forbidden man, because if she continued to let herself keep dwelling on his good looks or the size of his biceps in that short-sleeve shirt he was wearing . . . or the attractive way his hair was styled . . . or that devastating masculine after-shave he wore . . . well, it wouldn't be long before she would be entertaining some sort of idiotic, harebrained idea that they might . . . well, that would be totally ridiculous!

She was going back to New York in a few days, and by the time she got around to visiting Rueter Flats again, Luke would probably be married to Marilyn.

She threw her magazine down angrily.

Luke's gaze shot over to her expectantly as he slid the comb into the back pocket of his clean denims. "What's the matter?"

"Nothing." She stood up and smoothed her skirt nervously. "Are you ready to take me home?"

"No. Actually, I was thinking about making us an omelet," he said, grinning. He had no idea what had gotten her dander up, but suddenly she seemed to be on the defensive with him again. "How about it?"

"That isn't necessary," she refused crisply. "I can eat something when I get home."

"I can't see why you would want to do that when I've just offered to make your dinner," he chided.

Their eyes met stubbornly for a few moments and she felt herself weakening. She wanted to stay. She wanted to be with him—but she didn't want to be with him. Not when he was making her feel so confused, so uncertain. But time was growing short. Soon she would be gone.

"Oh, all right," she finally relented, mentally shaking herself for being so asinine about this. Luke had been the perfect gentleman all day and never once had he made any sort of pass at her. Her imagination or guilt for thinking such preposterous thoughts was her problem, not his.

She trailed along behind him, complaining to herself about the way his denims clinched his bottom so suggestively. No wonder the women in Rueter Flats drooled over him! His pants not only squeezed his bottom, but they were indecently tight in the front too. She had noticed that the minute he walked into the room.

Sure, he was a prize specimen of manhood. But did he have to advertise it so blatantly?

All of a sudden he stopped and she ran into the back of him. "Oh . . . I'm sorry," she mumbled.

"Did you say something?"

Oh, no, she hoped she hadn't been thinking out loud. "No." She grinned at him guiltily. "I didn't say anything."

They walked into the kitchen and he flipped on the lights. There was an island bar in the center of the room with various copper cookware hanging above it. Reaching for a large skillet, he placed it on the stove and busied himself dragging the ingredients for the omelets out of the refrigerator.

At his suggestion, she made the toast and brewed a pot of fresh coffee. The earlier tension began to dissolve as they sat down at the bar and ate their dinner, relaxing for the first time that day.

"I wonder if it's still raining?" she asked later as they leisurely sipped coffee in the den.

Luke was sitting at his desk, preparing to light an after-dinner cigar. "It was the last time I looked out."

She could see brief flashes of lightning illuminate the window behind his back as he began absently to sort through the day's mail. The fragrant smell of his cigar filled the room pleasantly and a feeling of lethargy stole over her. It felt uncommonly good to sit here with him and listen to the soft patter of rain outside the window.

"Do you live here alone?" she asked.

"No, I have a housekeeper and three other employees who help me run the ranch."

"The housekeeper lives here in the house with you?"

"No, I built a small guesthouse out back a few years ago. She lives there." He opened a long white envelope, briefly scanned the contents, then pitched it back on the desk.

She was curled up in the big old chair that sat before his desk and she began to grow warm and drowsy as he continued to read his mail. Before she knew what had happened, her eyes grew heavy and she began to nod.

Luke glanced up and a tender smile curved his lips as he observed her sleepy condition. The light from the lamp made her hair look shiny and lustrous and his fingers longed to touch the thick mass and see if it was as soft as he had imagined it to be.

She was slumped over like a child now, breathing softly as he pushed his chair back and stood up. She was exhausted and needed to be put to bed.

Walking around to the front of the desk, he knelt down beside her and reached out to gently awaken her when his hand paused.

Her skin had the flawless beauty that other women envy, and the subtle aroma of her perfume rose up to taunt him anew. Her face was warm and rosy and he felt his passion stirring, not for the first time that day. Of all the women he had known, she was the loveliest —and the most unobtainable.

He had no idea why he was torturing himself with thoughts of her, thoughts that were totally ridiculous. She had been on his mind both day and night since she had walked in Uriah's barn that day a little over three weeks ago. He could tell himself all he wanted that she was not the woman for him and that he'd better let well enough alone, but why was he constantly having to remind himself of that?

They were exact opposites. She loved her career and the big city, while he gloried in his work and small-town life. For one brief moment he let himself wonder what it would be like if they were actually to fall in love with one another.

His gaze lovingly ran over her again. It would never

work, Travers. Let it be. She seemed to be willing to coexist with him now without that constant sparring they had once indulged in. He would be a fool to try and change their relationship. If it wasn't for the fact that her father had taken ill, she would be back in New York, still detesting the ground Luke Travers walked upon. She was city and he was country and the two would mix like oil and water. He knew that.

He knew he would be walking down a blind alley if he ever once let himself touch her . . . hold her . . . kiss her. . . .

As if she could sense his presence, her eyes slowly opened and her brown eyes met his blue ones. "Umm . . . hi."

"Hello."

"Did I fall asleep?" He was kneeling beside her, so near she could smell his familiar scent, and it made her grow weak with desire.

"Yes. I guess you were tired." He knew this was the time to move away, to break this slender thread of intimacy that was threatening to draw them closer, but some invisible force rendered him powerless.

"You must be tired too." Her fingers reached out and lightly caressed his cheek and lingered there.

Fire raced unchecked through the nerve ends where her fingers touched. "Yes . . . a little," he confessed in a voice that had suddenly grown a little husky.

She gazed back at him sleepily, with eyes as warm and soft as a doe's. "Still raining?"

"Umm . . . still raining."

"Luke?"

"Umm?"

It would be dangerous and completely insane, but

she suddenly wanted this man to make love to her. She continued to gaze at him solemnly, searching for the right words to relay these lunatic, almost absurd feelings, but coming up depressingly empty-handed each time.

How do you tell a man you want him to make love to you?

After several long moments without speaking, his hand involuntarily reached out to stroke away a stray lock of her hair from the corner of her eye.

"Cass? Was there something you wanted to ask?"

The shyness had returned full-force, yet she reasoned if he wasn't going to make some sort of move, she would have to. It amazed her that he couldn't sense what she was asking.

"Cat got your tongue?" he prompted again teasingly.

She shook her head wordlessly, then slowly began pulling his mouth down to meet hers.

He looked at her vacantly for a moment, then comprehension began to sink in as he swore under his breath softly. "What is this . . . Cass . . . ?" Their mouths touched briefly and he felt his whole body go limp with desire.

"Rainy nights make me sort of . . . crazy," she excused lamely. It was a flimsy excuse, but she couldn't think of anything else to explain her sudden irrationality.

At first he thought he was dreaming, but when her hand began to pull him back to her once more, he went willingly, but by now his mind was whirling with indecision. What was he suppose to do now? If he ever once touched her, he was gone, and he knew it. So don't touch, Travers. Walk away before this gets out of hand. . . .

"Uh . . . yeah . . . they sort of have the same effect on me," he admitted, and kissed her again.

But his silent warnings went unheeded, and it seemed only too natural for the fleeting kisses they were temporarily exchanging to grow longer, deeper, more intense.

Sliding into the chair with her, he took her more fully into his arms and their mouths met hungrily. A few moments later he knew there would be no turning back. He would make love to her and he would enjoy every moment of it, no matter what tomorrow brought.

"Uh . . . Cass . . . do you want to . . . ?" He was still afraid to put words to what was taking place for fear it would all shatter in his face.

She nodded and nipped his lower lip seductively.

"Why?" His voice cracked nervously.

"Does there have to be a reason?" she prompted softly.

"I'm having a hard time understanding you," he confessed with an agonized groan. "At times you act as if I'm a leper and at others . . . well . . . what do you want from me? I'm only human, and if this is some little game you've decided to torture me with, I want to warn you you're playing with fire. I'm not the young boy you used to know who wouldn't dream of actually touching you because he held you in awe. I'm a man now, and I just might take what you're offering," he warned gruffly.

She laid her cheek against the rough palm of his

hand and gazed at him tenderly. "You never held me in awe," she chided.

"Yes, I did, and you knew it."

"I did not," she objected. "You always acted as if you couldn't stand me."

"I seem to recall it was the exact opposite. You were the one who couldn't stand me."

As long as he had brought up the subject, it seemed like a good time to confront him with a question that had nagged her for a long time now. "If that's the case, how come you took Sybil Wilson to that dance!"

He shrugged and replied cockily, "To get even with you for being such an uppity little snit." A slow grin tugged at the corners of his mouth. "Did that really bother you?"

"No . . . Well, yes, it did, come to think of it. It was terribly embarrassing to have you treat me that way in front of all our friends. I was miserable for days."

He chuckled and pressed his forehead tightly against hers. "I can't tell you how happy it makes me to hear you say that. I couldn't begin to tell you how many of my days you made miserable."

"You're terrible, but I must admit you're nothing like the Luke Travers I knew twelve years ago," she confessed, smoothly tracing the outline of his face with her fingertip.

"Is that a fact?" He captured her hand and brought it back to brush his mouth across the fingertips as the blue of his eyes deepened to an even darker hue. "Well, you're not exactly as I remembered you, either."

By his low, intimate tone, she knew it was the most sincere of compliments.

"Then why must you ask . . . why? We're two consenting adults now, accountable for our own actions."

"Because I don't think there could ever be any sort of commitment between us, Cass," he said raggedly. He knew that as well as she did.

"I'm not talking commitment," she teased as her fingers gently traced the outline of his nose, then his mouth, and paused as his lips closed over her fingertips once more.

"What if I were to say I'm not sure I could accept such an offer from you without a commitment?" he parried.

She lifted her eyes in disbelief. "Are you asking that of me?" She found it impossible to believe that he could be serious.

"No, of course not," he murmured, and Cass had the impression that question had slipped out unintentionally.

Her arms slid back around his neck invitingly. "Then you're just hedging. Do you want to make love to me or—"

His mouth closing over hers prevented her from finishing the sentence. Moments later, when their lips finally parted, he whispered against them suggestively, "I'll give you five minutes to reconsider your offer, then you're on your own."

"I don't need five minutes."

"Are you sure?"

"Let's just say I've always been fascinated by your unsavory reputation and I want to see if any of the gossip is true," she bargained, then grinned at him impishly. "But I hope you're aware a lot of people in this town have stripped you of your horns and tail and put a nice, neat little halo around your golden head."

"Don't worry. I've changed my morals," he comforted. "But not my technique."

"And apparently you're going to make me beg to see this miraculous transition," she breathed against the hollow of his throat.

"You're sure you want to see it?" he pressed.

Her arms tightened around his neck and their mouths came down to meet each other's eagerly. With a low groan, he slipped his arms beneath her and gently gathered her up against his chest. His mouth met hers once more, hard and demanding.

"Okay, lady. But remember, this was your idea," he cautioned a few moments later.

He carried her through the darkened living room and up the carpeted stairway, their mouths never leaving one another's for more than a moment.

She could not seem to get enough of the taste of him, or the smell, or the feel of him.

"I know this is shameless of me," she murmured, pressing warm kisses on his neck as they entered his bedroom. Like the rest of the house, it was decorated in tones of blues and browns. The large king-size bed dominated the room along with a highly polished oak armoire and dresser.

"You don't hear me complaining, do you?" he whispered against the sweetness of her mouth. "I just want you to be sure. . . ."

She pulled his mouth back down to meet hers in a kiss that put all his fears to rest as he lay her carefully on the bed, then lay down beside her.

"Luke, there really isn't any other woman in your

life right now, is there?" It seemed a little late to be inquiring about such matters, but it would shed a different light on what was about to happen.

"No. Is there someone special waiting for you back in New York?" He began to undress, watching her as they talked.

"No, I'm not involved with anyone . . . but about Marilyn?" She was afraid he wasn't being truthful with her.

He removed the last of his clothing and her breath caught. He was truly magnificent. "What about her?" he countered.

"Is it serious between the two of you?"

"If it was, I can assure you I wouldn't be standing here stark naked discussing her with you," he returned dryly.

"Then it isn't serious?" They were about to share an intimate moment, one that no doubt would be highly pleasurable, but it would change nothing in their relationship and she wouldn't think of letting him make love to her if he was involved with another woman.

He lay down beside her and began to kiss her, long and passionately, until all thoughts of anything or anyone else were completely obliterated from her mind.

Her hands buried in the golden dark blond hair that covered his chest as his hands slowly began to explore her.

Piece by piece, he removed her clothing, masterfully, skillfully, and with the breathtaking expertise she had expected.

"You are so beautiful," he whispered reverently. "So very beautiful." His mouth began an exploration of her body, his tongue touching and tasting, then lovingly kissing what until now had been the most forbidden of places.

"Methinks you haven't changed at all," she accused as her mind became increasingly muddled with the growing, sensual haze he was weaving.

He raised his head to look at her as the last obstacle of cloth was disposed of neatly and without ceremony. "You're too well practiced to be the saint you're reported to be," she scolded breathlessly.

"Naw, I'm just a real natural when it comes to this," he teased.

"Then you're exceedingly talented," she pointed out, trying to control an unexpected surge of jealousy. This was not the time to think about how he received his training, she reminded herself. A thirty-year-old man with Luke Travers's looks was not going to be completely celibate, even though that would have been extremely nice. . . .

"You're not bad yourself." He returned the compliment easily as he urged her hand to become more aggressively involved. He drew a sharp intake of breath as she willingly complied.

"It always amazes me how men take this sort of thing so . . . so casually," she pondered.

He groaned and rolled over and positioned her on top of his broad chest, his hands cupping her face gently. The feel of his masculinity against her bare stomach was a new and disturbing feeling for her. "Have you changed your mind about this?"

"Oh, no." After all, she shouldn't be blaming him for taking full advantage of something that she had instigated, yet it bothered her he had been almost . . . easy.

"Then can we discuss this at another time?" He ran the calloused tip of his thumb across her moist bottom lip, then lowered her lips back down to meet his with a hungry urgency.

"Luke, I think there's something you should know," she murmured against the pressure of his questing tongue.

"Later," he commanded in a voice that had grown weak with passion.

From that point on all conversation willingly ceased as he took full control of her reeling senses and began tutoring her in the joys of being Luke Travers's woman. He evoked new and provocative feelings within her, feelings that all too soon had them both crying for release from the exquisite torment that was threatening to consume them.

Later, as he became a part of her, he suddenly pulled away, a stunned look overtaking his passion-laden features. "Don't tell me . . ."

She shook her head mutely. "I tried to, but you wouldn't let me."

He was clearly aghast at the situation he now found himself in. "You mean you've never . . ."

"Well, it wasn't because I haven't had the opportunity," she quickly clarified. "It's just that I've never met a man I thought I wanted to do . . . this with . . ." her voice trailed off lamely.

Having been raised on a farm and watching the way the animals mated, she had convinced herself that a man would have to be something extremely special to warrant that sort of total involvement from her.

"You're thirty years old and never . . . well . . . you should have stopped me. . . ." He immediately began to move away, but she determinedly pulled his lips back down to meet hers. "If you stop, I'll never speak to you again, Luke Travers."

By that time the issue was a useless one, anyway. It was far too late to discuss the advisability of what was taking place. His unexpected discovery only served to add prudence to a smoldering inferno that quickly recaptured precedence over all.

Later, as they lay in each other's arms, satiated and incredibly relaxed, Cassie thought she could finally understand why her sisters were so darn happy and optimistic all the time.

If the men of Rueter Flats were anything like Luke, she had been bad-mouthing them unjustly.

"Are you asleep?" she murmured drowsily. She was lying on her side, pressed tightly against the warmth of his back. The rain was falling harder again outside, the low rumble of thunder periodically breaking the silence. She should be getting up and going home, but somehow she wanted to lengthen the time she had with him.

"No, just thinking."

"About what?"

"About you." He rolled over and reached for his shirt beside the bed and withdrew a cigar. Propping himself up on a pillow, he lit the thin cylinder and then drew her into the crook of his arm. "That was a dirty thing to do to a man."

"I tried to tell you. You said, 'Later.' "

"I wouldn't have said 'later' if I'd known that was what you were trying to tell me," he protested.

"You could have stopped," she pointed out.

He raised a brow in patient tolerance as he drew on

143

the cigar and let the smoke curl around their heads in a blue cloud. "Right."

She smiled and impishly traced her finger around his bare navel. "Are you saying you're sorry for what happened?"

"No . . . but I should be," he admitted.

"No you shouldn't. I was the one who started it."

"That doesn't make any difference." He inhaled again and looked over at her, then a wicked, devilish grin she had seen a million times before broke out on his face. "I was really the first, huh?"

She smiled back at him. "Yeah . . . why I picked you, I don't know," she teased. They both would have readily admitted that Luke Travers would seem like a highly unlikely candidate for Cass McCason's favors.

"It was a hell of a shock," he confided.

"Why?"

"Well, I thought with you moving away and all there had probably been numerous men in your life."

"No, not intimately anyway. I know it's highly unusual for a woman my age to be inexperienced in these matters, and I have dated a lot of men. I'll even confess there was one time that I came close to letting a man make love to me, but I backed out," she confessed sheepishly.

"At the last moment?" Luke shook his head in sympathy for the poor man. "I bet that made his day."

"No, he wasn't very happy about it, but it wasn't right for me and I realized it in time. I have always promised myself that that's how it would have to be before I could let that happen."

Luke gazed at her thoughtfully. "And tonight was right for you?"

144

She smiled. "Tonight was very right for me," she affirmed softly, then sighed and pressed a kiss on his bare stomach. "And maybe I'm a little bit old-fashioned too. Throw it all in together and you have a thirty-year-old virgin, like it or not."

Luke instinctively pulled her closer and tilted her face up so he could give her another long kiss. When their lips parted several moments later he smiled at her tenderly, his voice strangely emotional now. "There's nothing wrong with a woman being old-fashioned. Thank you, Cass. That's the nicest gift I've ever had."

Cassie felt her heart overflowing with something suspiciously close to love as she smiled back at him. "My pleasure, Dr. Travers." By referring to him as a doctor, it was as close as she had ever come to letting him know she was terribly proud of him.

He bowed his head to her respectfully. "No, it was all mine, Ms. McCason."

Ms. McCason? She grinned.

She thought they finally understood each other.

CHAPTER NINE

Had she been wiser, she would have realized that the blissful hours she was spending in Luke's company could only complicate a situation that was already out of hand.

She had no intention of becoming seriously involved with a man from Rueter Flats, even though a certain veterinarian's electrifying kisses and captivating smiles were capable of making her a blithering idiot at times. Already he was occupying her thoughts far more than he should be, and events were moving along entirely too fast to suit her.

It seemed like every spare minute they could find in the following days they would immediately seek out each other's presence, whether it was to take Wylie to a movie or on a fishing expedition, or the times that she secretly enjoyed the most, when she and Luke would sneak away for a few stolen moments of their own.

Their relationship was reckless and exciting and a totally unthinkable one, and yet they never spoke about their new feelings for fear they would have to do something about them.

The three had gone to a rodeo one night and spent

the entire time eating hot dogs and cotton candy and laughing. It seemed like she could laugh so much easier with Luke than she could anyone else.

And another time she had coerced him into accompanying her on a shopping expedition to find Uriah a new recliner. Her father's favorite chair was old and worn out, and Cassie wanted to buy something new and more comfortable for him when he returned home, although Luke warned that Uriah would not give up the old chair without a fight.

The church had its shiny new piano now. Luke and Cassie had selected the instrument with care. Luke insisted on donating it to the church in honor of Uriah and Neoma McCason, and Cassie's heart was touched.

Morgan Pixley sat in his pew Sunday mornings and beamed with pleasure as the Widow Neely played the old hymns in clear, resounding tones. In a way it seemed like he was much happier that Louella's piano wasn't there to remind him of happier days.

Luke, Cassie, and Wylie attended services together and then on Sunday afternoons, much to her surprise, he took her up in his small plane. They flew around Rueter Flats and Macon while he pointed out every landmark in the area to her.

On those afternoons her attention was diverted from sight-seeing because she enjoyed watching the pilot more than the sights! She had never acted this way around a man before and she was at a loss as to why she had suddenly picked Luke Travers to become so infatuated with.

If she was going to go off the deep end, why couldn't it be with one of the men she knew in New York? Tony

Jackson or Ed Flannery or Larry Ellison—or anyone but Luke.

It was really quite senseless to be so giddy about him. She reminded herself of that a hundred times a day, but it didn't seem to do any good because her pulse still raced like a sixteen-year-old's and her knees still turned to jelly every time he walked into the room.

She was in the process of giving herself another stern mental shakedown concerning Luke as she mucked out the stalls in the barn Wednesday morning. She had been home a little over five weeks, and every day she could feel herself growing a little closer to him.

This is exactly how the women of Rueter Flats get in their predicaments, she warned. They meet a good-looking man and before they know what hit them, Wham! they're on their way to the altar, then on to the local maternity ward.

Well, not her.

She would be leaving any day now. She would look back on this time for what it was—a pleasant interlude with a man she would no doubt always remember. When she returned home periodically she would speak to him when they bumped into each other at local gatherings, but that's as far as it would go.

By then he would be married. Her thoughts skidded to a screeching halt at the unpalatable prediction. Well, maybe not. It wasn't unheard of for a man to remain a bachelor.

Luke and Wylie entered the barn as she was still trying to convince herself of that feeble possibility. His gaze was unwillingly drawn to the way her tight jeans hugged her bottom. She was wearing another one of those clinging T-shirts that dipped low at her neckline and fit snugly to her breasts. She had acquired a smooth, even tan from working outdoors the past few weeks and a fine sheen of perspiration lay on her skin. Her face was flushed from the mounting heat and her hair was mussed and full of bits of hay, but she was still able to send his blood boiling to a fever pitch.

He had lain awake every night for hours the past few nights torturing himself with the remembrance of her in his arms, unbelievably soft and giving, unbelievably his. . . .

He would only be kidding himself if he thought anything serious could ever come out of their brief affair. But the searing memory of that rainy night still wielded the power to make him toss and turn between tumbled sheets until the wee hours of morning.

Why couldn't Marilyn make him feel this way? He would agonize as his new feelings continued to bewilder him. It seemed with increasing regularity that he was watching yet another dawn break peacefully outside his bedroom window. Marilyn was beautiful and talented and had no thoughts of leaving Macon in search of greener pastures. They could have a good life together. Even though they had never discussed the subject of marriage, Luke knew she would welcome his proposal, and yet for some reason he had always held back.

And he had no idea why he continued to delay. He was thirty years old, his practice was growing every day, and he wanted to get married and settle down. He could think of nothing that he would want more than a wife to come home to every night—a woman he could hold in his arms and share all the pent-up love he had kept so carefully hidden from the world with— a woman who could set his senses on fire and turn his insides to mush, one who he could argue with, make up with, share his dreams with, grow old with. . . .

His eyes followed the woman raking hay with reckless abandon and he felt an overwhelming sense of frustration wash over him. A woman like Cassie, dammit! Even if she was stubborn as a jackass at times!

This morning had been set aside for fishing, and Luke was sorely tempted to send Wylie on to the river by himself and spend a few moments alone with her, but he quickly checked his thoughts. After yet another interrupted night's sleep last night he had promised himself that he was going to have to begin cooling it where Cass was concerned. It was hopeless between them, and he'd better get used to the idea.

The redolent smells of hay and manure filled the air as her pitchfork paused in midair when she spotted him. She broke out into a radiant smile. "Hi!"

Against his will, his face had that same illumination as he grinned slowly back at her. "Hi."

"I suppose you guys are ready to go fishing, but I'm afraid I won't be able to go with you. I'm only half through with my work," she confessed. If she hadn't spent so much time daydreaming about him, she would have finished long ago.

"Okay," Wylie accepted easily. "Me and Luke will go ahead and you can bring us some sandwiches later on."

Cass frowned. "Thanks a lot."

Luke chuckled and reached for the extra pitchfork leaning against one of the stalls. "Why don't you go on down to the river and I'll help your sister finish up in here?"

It was Wylie who frowned this time. "Aw, Luke. Can't she finish it herself?"

Luke swatted him playfully on his behind and gave him a gentle nudge out the doorway. "We'll be down in about an hour. I want to see at least two big old flatheads on your stringer when I get there."

"Oh, all right. But be sure and bring plenty of sandwiches and cookies when you come." Wylie was back to his old self after the time he had spent with Uriah, but he was still grumbling something under his breath about "girls" as he headed for the river.

With two of them working, the stalls were soon tidied up and the tack room was put back in order. Luke was transporting sacks of grain to the storage room when Cassie began to feel playful. She had watched the way his powerful muscles bunched enticingly across his broad back as he lifted the heavy sacks and transported them into another room. He had stripped off his shirt in the intense heat and sweat now rolled in wet rivulets off his bronzed body and dampened the thick blond hair on his chest.

It took very little for her mind to conjure up what it felt like to be held tightly against that soft mass and the feel of it tangled beneath her fingers. . . . Her mind continued to torture her with the remembrance of the feel of those muscles, firm and bare beneath her fingertips. She bit her lower lip thoughtfully, then leaned over and waited for him to walk past the loft again.

When he did she pitched a huge forkful of hay down on his head.

Shifting the bundle more evenly on his shoulder, he glanced up and shot her a warning look. "I would watch that if I were you."

She smiled at him prettily. "Ooops, sorry. My fork just slipped."

But when he carried another sack by a few minutes later, another forkful of hay bombarded him.

Glancing up once more, he paused and carefully sat the sack down at his feet. Hooking his thumbs in the loops of his jeans, he leveled his blue gaze on her sternly. "Are you lookin' for trouble, lady?"

"Heavens no! I don't know why I'm so clumsy today," she apologized, a tiny grin threatening to give her away. She lay in the loft hanging over the side, looking at him invitingly. "You have hay all down your back," she divulged sympathetically.

He shifted his weight to one leg impatiently. "Yes, I'd noticed that."

"Bet it's miserable, huh?"

"You got it." He reached down and hefted the sack of grain back to his shoulder and carried it on into the storage room.

She shrugged, deciding he wasn't going to take the bait, and resignedly turned back to her work. She could hear water running outside a few moments later and she peaked out the loft door, but she couldn't see him anywhere.

The next thing she knew a whirlwind of hay came swirling through the air and literally engulfed her. She yelped and lost her footing as a heavy object came hurtling toward her.

"Luke Travers! I'm going to murder you!" She tried to sound authoritative but she was laughing too hard.

"Ooops, pardon me," he mocked. "I don't know why I'm so clumsy today." He cupped the back of her neck and started to kiss her as their legs became entangled and they fell in a heap on the hay. She started to giggle as he momentarily forgot the kiss and began energetically stuffing hay down her pants.

"You stop that this minute!" she sputtered as she tried to slap his hands away from the snap on her jeans. In addition to stuffing hay, they were becoming awfully familiar!

"Make me," he taunted as another handful of hay plummeted down the front of her T-shirt.

They tumbled over and over in the sweet-smelling hay as she tried to free herself of his mighty hold, but it soon became apparent she was no match for his strength.

Not even if she had wanted to be . . . which she didn't.

She couldn't deny that it felt wonderful to be pressed up tightly against him again, to touch him, to smell him, to feel his bare chest molded next to hers. Scooping up a handful of hay, she rammed it down the front of his pants and heard him suck in his breath as she encountered more than they both had bargained for.

He hurriedly rolled over and pinned her flat, all the while keeping her hand firmly trapped in place. He gazed down at her, his eyes deepening to the dark, passionate hue she had seen one time before, and she smiled up at him lamely. "Take that, you big bully."

He grinned wickedly. "Gladly."

She blushed and pushed at him ineffectually for a few moments, then finally shrugged and with her one free hand pulled his mouth slowly down to meet hers. "Well, if you're going to enjoy yourself so darn much, I might as well join you."

Their mouths touched briefly as he murmured unevenly against her lips. "Are you wanting something?" he teased as he ran the tip of his tongue lightly over her bottom lip.

"What you got to offer, sugggaarrr?" she teased back in a long Texas drawl.

"For you?" He growled suggestively, then playfully nipped her lower lip with gentle roughness. "Anything you want."

And once again their earlier avowals of prudence and temperance and all those other promises they had adamantly made to themselves went up in a puff of smoke.

Cassie wasn't sure how it happened, but it seemed their clothes were shed with alarming swiftness. She vaguely remembered murmuring a soft protest that someone might see them, but her protests were met with another mind-boggling kiss.

"Close the loft door," he murmured between kisses.

"But, Luke . . . it's broad daylight," she protested once more, but it was hard to sound very convincing . . . not when she reached out and slammed the door to the loft herself.

And then he made love to her again.

Not in the tender, almost reverent way he had the first time, but with a seemingly pent-up passion that was turbulent, restless, hungry, and yet so incredibly gentle.

Only this time he took the time to introduce her to the pleasures of pleasing a man, and when his lessons

154

were readily learned she became almost giddy to find out she could weaken such a strong man to the point where he lay slack and drained of strength in her arms. She placed sultry kisses over his smooth, taut skin, and discovered anew the treasure of his lean, brown body, toughened by hard work and nature's elements.

And then when he could stand no more of her exquisite torture, he turned her over on her back and began his own virile assault, one of teasing and arousing to the point of madness, then dropping back to arouse and tease once more until she begged for fulfillment.

"Oh, Cass." He hated this feeling of such helplessness when he was in her arms. She was like no other woman he had ever known . . . searing his senses, invading his mind, penetrating his heart until he wanted to cry out for her to stop, to have mercy.

But instead he only muffled her cries with his own as their senses exploded in a brilliant shower of wild delirium while the sensations went on and on and on. . . .

When the fiery storm finally abated, he held her in his arms and buried his face in her hair, drained of strength, yet feeling strangely alive and vibrant.

"I don't know how that happened . . . but it was wonderful," she murmured as she sighed and snuggled closer to him.

The heat was so intense inside the loft they could barely breathe, and yet neither one made an effort to move.

Bits of hay were stuck in their hair and their bodies glistened with a fine sheen and still they stayed locked in one another's arms.

"I don't either." Luke kissed her again softly. "I didn't want this to happen again, Cass."

She felt a sharp twinge at his admission. She hadn't planned on it either, and yet now that it had happened, she didn't regret it. "You mean . . . you regret it?"

"No . . . not regret." He would never regret what they had shared. "I . . . I guess I really don't know what I mean," he sighed.

It wasn't hard to understand his confusion. She had plenty of her own.

"I know. Sometimes I wonder how this all started, don't you?" They lay together in the loft, gazing up at a patch of blue sky that was showing through the tin roof.

"Yeah, it is strange, isn't it? Luke Travers and Cassie McCason." They rolled their heads to one side and grinned at each other knowingly.

"Unlikely combination, huh?"

"Oh, I don't know." He reached over and caressed her cheek thoughtfully. "I'd say we weren't all that bad together."

"No, not bad at all," she agreed.

But he knew that no matter how wonderful this afternoon had been, he wouldn't be doing it again. The whole relationship was just becoming too painful for him. While he couldn't deny she shared the depth of his passion, he didn't dare let himself hope that she was falling in love with him.

And for some reason, that tore at his heart, because he was in love with her.

As crazy as that was, he could no longer shove the fact aside and pretend it didn't exist. It did exist. But as strong as his love was, he wasn't about to confess it to her for fear she would laugh at him the way she had when they were young and remind him this was only a summer fling. Surely he would be the last man she would actually fall in love with.

He couldn't stand that.

He raised his eyes to meet hers and they stared into each other's depths for long moments before he sighed again and admitted, "You're a hell of a woman, Cass."

She ran one finger lightly across his full lower lip. "Thank you, sir."

She waited, breathlessly hoping he would mention the word *love,* yet praying he wouldn't. Because if he did, she honestly didn't know what she would say to him.

It was becoming increasingly hard to think about a life without Luke Travers in it, and yet what could she do? Move back to Rueter Flats? At one time the thought would have been laughable, but that was before the last two weeks had occurred. Could she actually entertain the thought of giving up a successful career with an impending promotion just for the chance to be near him?

The thought was ludicrous, and yet she found herself frantically sorting through what few alternatives there would be if she did decide to do anything that frivolous. She supposed she could always find a job in Macon, but it wouldn't be doing what she loved. And what made her think that just because she was having these crazy feelings toward him that he returned them? He had never indicated that he was in love with her. Far from it. He seemed to avoid any talk of personal involvement. Not even at the pinnacle of his passion had he ever murmured the words *I love you, Cass,* yet they had been on the tip of her tongue more than once.

Yet the way he was looking at her now, with such longing . . . such . . . well, if it wasn't love she was seeing, then she was at a loss to describe what it could be. Maybe, just maybe if he would bring up the subject of their growing relationship, then she could admit she was beginning to care for him. . . .

But he didn't mention the word.

Not then as they were getting dressed or later as he helped her make sandwiches for the delayed fishing trip.

She could only assume the word had never occurred to him, and it was a stunning revelation to her.

It was late afternoon when they cleaned the fish they had caught and Cassie put them in the freezer for Uriah to enjoy when he returned home.

She walked out to the truck with Luke to say good-bye, trying to appear casual in front of Wylie. "It's still early. You could stay for supper," she invited. "I'd even fix macaroni and cheese." It was another one of his favorites and she hoped to entice him into staying.

"I'd love to." He smiled at her and that strange light came into his eyes once more. "But I can't."

"Big date tonight," she teased lightly, praying that he would say that was not the case.

"Just with a sick horse."

"Oh." She knew she sounded unduly relieved, but at this point she didn't really care. "You going to the party the Murphys are throwing tomorrow night?"

"I was planning on it. How about you?"

"I thought I would. Dad should be coming home day after tomorrow and I'll be leaving. The party will give me a chance to say good-bye to everyone," she finished hurriedly.

At the mention of her departure, Luke turned and opened the truck door, then asked in a short voice, "You want to ride to the party with me?"

"Yes, I'd like that."

"Fine. I'll pick you up around seven." He got in the truck and slammed the door sharply.

"I'll be waiting."

It seemed like it took unusually long for seven o'clock to come around the following evening, but Cassie was dressed and sitting on the porch waiting for him when he finally arrived.

Her first impulse was to run over and shower him with kisses as he got out of his truck, but she quickly quelled the urge.

She would wait and see how he greeted her.

"Hi."

"Hi." He walked up and paused, his eyes inspecting her lazily. She was wearing a white cotton sundress with some pretty pink embroidered flowers around the neckline. Her shoulders were bare again, displaying the dark tan she had acquired, and he marveled anew at how beautiful she was.

"You look nice," he complimented.

"Thank you. You do too." He had to mean it, because he was looking at her as if she had just been declared the winner in a wet T-shirt contest.

The evening was to be another informal gathering, so he had dressed accordingly. Denims and a blue checked Western shirt, yet he was as devastatingly handsome as if he had been wearing a black tie and tuxedo.

"Ready?" He offered his arm and she stood up and placed her hand in it.

"Ready."

They strolled out to his truck and she paused and grinned at him knowingly. "Want to take the Jag?"

He pretended to have to think the suggestion over, but she knew what his answer was going to be. He was dying to drive that car. "Sure, why not," he finally agreed with an indifferent shrug.

He was in the car in a flash, busy inspecting all the gauges and accessories the car came equipped with before she could get in the passenger side.

"You big faker. You've been dying to get your hands on this, haven't you?" she accused as she snapped on her seat belt. He turned the key in the ignition and shifted down into low, then gave her a sexy wink.

He wasn't fooling her one bit with this so-what-if-it's-a-Jaguar act.

She could see boyish anticipation written all over his face.

But her words were drowned out as her head snapped back and the high squeal of rubber meeting pavement rent the air.

They blasted out onto the highway like a rocket and he began to wind the motor out until they were careening down the highway like a silver bullet.

She could honestly say it was the fastest trip she had ever made to the Murphys—or anywhere else—in her life.

When they finally zoomed up the drive she let out a huge sigh of relief and snatched the keys out of the ignition the minute they rolled to a stop. "You just see if I ever let you drive again!"

He looked at her solemnly. "You realize it's a little doggy."

"Doggy!"

He grinned and leaned over to kiss her. "Okay. I'll admit it. You've got a nice car, and I'm envious as hell."

"Good. It's been a long time comin'." She returned his kiss with full measure, which consequently delayed their arrival by another ten minutes.

They were greeted enthusiastically when they entered. Most of Cassie's brothers and sisters were there with their husbands and wives, all except Rowena and her family, who had decided to take Wylie and go to the county fair instead.

The party turned out to be a boisterous one. Sawyer Middleton spotted her immediately and claimed the first few dances as his.

Luke smiled and handed her over willingly, but Cassie thought he seemed disappointed that they wouldn't have the first dance.

By the time the small band swung into the third number, Cassie was pleading mercy and Sawyer promptly escorted her over to old washtubs iced down with beer and soft drinks. "What's your pleasure?"

She chose a soft drink and he peeled off the tab and handed her a bright red can. Seth Holoson stopped by to ask for a dance later, and she motioned with her free hand that she would be available as she took a long, refreshing drink.

"Good boy, that Holoson," Sawyer commented as

he ripped the tab off a beer and took a long swallow. "Make someone a fine husband."

She smiled and took another sip of her drink. Sawyer was a born matchmaker, but you would think with his less than perfect record with women, he would look for another hobby.

"When I was over in Macon the other day I stopped by the hospital and visited with your daddy. Said he might be comin' home soon."

"Yes, tomorrow."

"That soon? Well, that's just great!"

"It is wonderful, isn't it? The doctor says he should be as good as new if he'll take care of himself."

"Well, we'll all just have to make sure he does." Sawyer leveled his gaze on her sternly. "You give any more thought to what we talked about the other day?"

He could tell she hadn't by the way she grinned back at him sheepishly.

"I thought so. Well, little lady, you're makin' a big mistake by not givin' it some serious consideration," he warned.

"Sawyer, I can't visualize me opening my own agency," Cassie protested. "That takes a lot of money and I'm afraid I spend mine as fast as I make it."

"Missy." Sawyer had obviously never heard of the ERA. He "missyed, "little womaned," and "honeyed" every woman he met. "Any bank around here would be itchin' to loan you the money if you went to them with two or three big accounts already in your pocket," he insisted.

"But I don't have two or three accounts already in my pocket," she argued.

"Well, you could have if you'd get busy! I saw Wally

Henson and Oscar Miller over at the Elks Club last night and we got to talking about how hard it was to get good advertisin'—you remember Wally and Oscar, don't you, honey? Wally owns the poultry plant over in Macon and Oscar owns that big fleet of semis."

She nodded patiently.

"Well, they said to tell you they were sick of dealing with these eggheads around here and they'd sure be glad to throw their business your way if you decide to open up your own agency. There's your three accounts right there."

Her gaze unwillingly found itself centered on Luke again as Sawyer droned on. He was dancing with one of the younger girls in the crowd and she had to smother a smile to see how mesmerized she was. He was charming and handsome and totally capable of capturing any woman's heart, no matter what their age.

"Throw in the fact that Uriah and Neoma would plumb be beside themselves if you'd come on back home, I can't see what you're waitin' for, sugar," Sawyer challenged.

Pulling her gaze away from Luke, she smiled and started to explain to Sawyer about her upcoming promotion with Creble and Associates when Seth came back to claim her for his dance.

Cassie gave Sawyer an apologetic smile as he led her back to the dance floor, yet she was relieved to have the discussion interrupted.

The idea of opening her own agency was ridiculous, yet for some reason she did find herself tucking it in the back of her mind to give more serious thought to later on.

For the next hour she danced and laughed and forgot all about illnesses and advertising agencies and the endless decisions that suddenly seemed to be raining down upon her.

The only incident to mar the evening was when she came back into the room after catching a breath of fresh air with Bray Williams and found Luke dancing with Marilyn. It was a slow, romantic waltz and it made Cassie feel as if she were coming unglued.

To see Marilyn in his arms had a devastating effect on her and she couldn't keep her eyes off the attractive couple as Bray whirled her around the floor.

They smiled at each other as they brushed shoulders on the dance floor and Cassie fought to keep her expression pleasant.

"Hi. Having a nice time?"

Luke grinned at her, one of those sexy suggestive grins he was so good at leveling at her when he wanted to irritate. "Great. How about you?"

"Great."

Later, as he pulled her into his arms without even asking, she wanted to pull away and make him miserable for a while! But as their bodies blended in heavenly reunion, she found herself nestling much closer than was required.

"Are you still enjoying yourself?" she inquired nicely.

"It just got better." He winked. "How about you?"

"Yes, I'm having fun," she replied coolly. "How is Marilyn?"

"At what?" he asked innocently.

She eyed him sternly. "Dancing."

"Oh. She's just fine. How is Seth?

"He's just fine."

"And Bray?"

"Fine . . ."

"And Ron?"

He had made his point.

"Fine! She looks lovely tonight."

"Who?"

"Marilyn!"

He angled himself around until he could see the petite blonde, who was dancing in Brad Younger's arms now. "Yeah, she does, doesn't she." He glanced down at her warily as she inched even closer.

Her eyes narrowed and she slid her arms around his neck possessively. "I don't think she looks all that good."

"Well, you just said she did. . . . Uh . . . you mind to tell me what you're doing?" he groaned miserably as her suggestive actions began to affect him.

She had an uncanny way of arousing him to such a fevered pitch and getting him there in record time that he was afraid it could get mighty embarrassing for him at any moment if she kept this up.

"I'm just dancing close to you like Marilyn was," she murmured, but she wanted to make it perfectly clear to whoever happened to be watching that she was staking her claim.

"She wasn't dancing this close to me," he denied swiftly.

"It certainly looked that way to me!"

"Cass, look"—He carefully maneuvered her away from him to a more comfortable distance—"I think if you're going to make a pass at me, which I have no objections to," he assured hurriedly, "don't you think we'd enjoy it more if we found a little more privacy than a crowded dance floor?"

"Am I embarrassing you?" She was pressing so tightly now he was beginning to perspire heavily.

He groaned and pushed her back again to a safer distance. "No, I'd say torturing would be a better word."

She smiled smugly as she felt the ever-growing evidence of his words pressed against her middle. "You don't care if Marilyn gets the wrong idea about us?"

"Marilyn? Is that what all this is about?" He paused and looked at her with annoyance.

"Well, for someone who isn't serious about someone, you sure looked like you were having a good time a minute ago."

"Me! What did I do?"

"Pasted yourself to her, that's what!"

"Well, if I remember correctly, you and Seth weren't exactly dancing like brother and sister," he returned curtly.

"Me—Seth," she sputtered. "We were merely dancing. You and Marilyn were . . . were . . ."

"Dancing!" he supplied stubbornly, then set their feet back in motion. "You're making a scene," he grumbled. "I was only dancing with Marilyn because you weren't available."

"When did you ask?"

"I never got the chance. You were always occupied!" He glanced around uneasily and found that people were beginning to stare. "Let's just drop the subject, okay?"

"I'm not making a scene. I only pointed out that you look like you were enjoying yourself."

"Well, I'm sorry. Okay? Next time I'll try to snarl and frown and look perfectly miserable the whole time I'm dancing with her."

"The next time you dance with her I won't be here to see it," she snapped, and her words sliced deeply within both of them.

"I'm fully aware of that," he said calmly. "You don't have to keep reminding me."

They danced in strained silence for a moment, then she said in a more appeasing tone, "I know I've been taking up a lot of your time lately with the farm and all, and I know it's been because of Dad that you've helped me the way you have, but I want to thank you for all your help. I know I've interfered with your personal life, and now that I'm leaving, you can get back to normal." She paused and warned herself not to say it, but she went ahead anyway. "I suppose you'll probably have more time to spend with your friends when I leave."

"I haven't been neglecting any of my friends," he denied.

"You mean you've been seeing . . . her . . . while I've been here?" That thought nearly killed her. He had made love to her, then still dated Marilyn!

He heaved a long, put-upon sigh. "Now who in the hell may I ask is 'her'?"

"Marilyn!"

"Oh for heaven's sake! No. I haven't been seeing her." You would think by the way she was acting she would actually be offended if he dated another woman.

"Oh." She realized she was being a little pushy. After all, he could see who he wanted. She had no strings attached to him. But she was curious as to what he would be doing after she left. He had obviously spent every spare moment he had with her since Uriah had taken ill. "Well, not that it matters, but I was only trying to find out what you were going to do with all your time after I leave."

For a long time he didn't answer her and she thought perhaps he was only being stubborn again, but then he buried his face in the cradle of her neck and confessed in a very small voice, "I don't know what I'll do when you leave, Cass." Then as quickly as he had lost it, he regained his composure and added more firmly, "I make it a point to live one day at a time," he stated curtly.

It wasn't what he said but rather the way he said it that made her suddenly want to cry. No matter how she had felt about him in the past, she didn't feel that way about him now. The Luke she had come to know seemed so vulnerable that she wanted to fold him in her arms and keep him forever.

For a brief moment he had actually sounded as if he would miss her. But that was crazy. All he would have to do is tell her what he was feeling and then she would gladly confess her love.

"I . . . I can't thank you enough for being with me these past few weeks, Luke." Her own voice was a little unsteady now as she continued in a gentle tone, "I don't know what I would have done without you." Her hands tightened in his hair and she closed her eyes painfully as he moved her closer to him. She was giving him every chance to open up to her.

But the moments passed and, other than a perceptible tightening of his arms around her, he said nothing.

She choked back the tears and decided the only

good and noble thing to do at this point was to wish him the very best of luck, but it was like trying to squeeze blood out of a turnip to get the words past her dry lips. "And I just want to say that I . . . hope you and whoever you choose to marry will be very happy. . . ."

He finally paused and looked down at her for a very long time, then suddenly began to maneuver her off the dance floor.

Amid her confused protests, he pulled her out onto the terrace, where he pushed solidly up against a vine-covered wall that was in the darkest corner of the building and trapped her between his two arms. "You know what your problem is?"

She looked at him worriedly. "No, what?"

"You talk too much." He then proceeded to kiss her until she went limp as a rag in his arms.

"My goodness, what brought this on?" she managed when she was finally able to catch her breath.

He sighed and stole another smoldering kiss before he answered. When he spoke he dropped a bomb she wasn't expecting. "I wanted to be alone with you when we said good-bye."

"Good-bye? What do you mean, good-bye? I don't leave until Saturday."

"I know, but I figure there'll be a lot of confusion around your place when Uriah comes home, and be-sides that, I have to fly over to Seeny County sometime tomorrow to tend to business." The tips of his thumbs gently caressed her mouth, which was slightly swollen from his ardent kisses. "I want to say good-bye to you now, Cass."

For a long time they stared at each other in the

moonlight, both at a complete loss for words. There were so many things they wanted to say to one another, and yet they were afraid.

Afraid the other one would laugh if they would dare confess that Luke Travers loved Cassie McCason or Cassie McCason loved Luke Travers.

"John said he would drop me by your place later so I can pick up my truck. And he has a heifer he wants me to take a look at before I leave tonight."

"But, Luke . . ." She wasn't even going to have these last few precious hours with him because John Murphy had a sick cow!

"I . . . let's just make this as easy as possible, Cass." His eyes pleaded with her for understanding, yet she didn't know what she was supposed to understand. "Can't you stop in later? Wylie is staying all night with Rowena. You could stay with me tonight," she offered, casting all pride aside now.

"Thanks, but it will probably be too late." It was going to be hard enough to walk off and leave her. One more precious night would only add salt to an already gaping wound. He gazed at her lovingly as he smoothed back a stray lock of hair from her face, trying to memorize everything about her so that after tonight he could hold her in his heart if not in his arms.

God, how he loved her. Oh, she made him mad as hell at times, and yet she could make him feel emotions that no other woman had ever been able to. He supposed deep down he'd always loved her, even when they were children. But she was no more obtainable to him now than she had been then. What was it she had

170

said the first time he had made love to her—she wasn't looking for a commitment?

His mind churned with confusion. It would be so easy to tell her that he loved her, to confess that if she would marry him it would make him the happiest man on earth, that he would go out of his way to make sure she would have that same happiness, even though she would be living back in Rueter Flats. But he knew without asking she would never settle for that kind of life.

And he could never uproot his life and move to New York.

So it was best to end it now, swiftly and cleanly, while he still had a small remnant of sanity left in him.

He kissed her once more, long and passionately, then raised his head and touched his nose to hers affectionately, then whispered softly, "See you around, kid."

"Luke . . ." She was so confused and miserable, she thought her heart would break. That was it? After all they had shared together he was going to walk out of her life with a simple "See you around, kid"?

But her silent plea went unanswered as he quickly turned and left her standing in the shadows, alone and lonely, feeling as if part of her had just died.

CHAPTER TEN

Many thoughts raced through Cassie's mind as she drove to New York.

As predicted, Uriah's homecoming was boisterous and happy and sad all at the same time.

Happy because he was home and recovering from the stroke nicely, but sad for his children to realize that no longer could they think of their parents as being invincible. It would seem nature had a way of pointing that out when it was least expected.

For Cassie it was a more emotional time than it was for the others. She hated to leave the safety and love of her parents' home, and yet she knew she had another life waiting for her when she returned to New York.

And Luke. How in the world had she allowed herself to fall in love with him?

She still bristled when she thought about the way he had chosen to say good-bye to her. She had felt confident that he would change his mind and come to see her before she actually left. There were too many unsaid things between them for him to end it this way.

But he hadn't come by to see her and she had been too stubborn to call him, so consequently she was still angrily jerking tissues out of a box and wiping at the relentless stream of tears when she entered the city limits of New York on Monday evening.

The apartment smelled musty as she let herself in and switched on the air conditioner. There was a pile of papers and a stack of mail on her kitchen counter, left for her by her cleaning woman. She looked around her and everything was the same.

Except nothing was the same at all.

She was exhausted from crying halfway across the United States so she went directly to the shower, then fell into bed. She was sure she would quickly shed this miserable feeling of despondency the moment she returned to her office tomorrow morning.

It was going to leave anytime now, she continued to remind herself as her life gradually settled back into a routine pattern. She couldn't go on forever mooning over a man who apparently didn't care one whit for her. She had known Luke Travers was trouble from the day he had tied her braids in a knot when they were in the first grade.

She stood in her office staring down at the traffic late one Thursday afternoon when she had been back at work almost three weeks. It was the height of rush hour and she was glad to have a desk piled high with work. She planned on working late tonight, as she had done almost every night since she returned. It wasn't that she couldn't get caught up, it just gave her a reasonable excuse to be away from the apartment. The nights were far too lonely now, and she had found herself calling home at least three times a week to check on her father. She had asked about Luke each time, and Neoma had told her they hadn't seen as much of him as they usually did.

Then she had lain awake all night wondering just what he was doing that took up so much of his time!

Her gaze was drawn to the west, where the sun was a blazing red ball of fire. It was just beginning to sink behind the tall skyscrapers and she was reminded of the way the sun sat in Rueter Flats.

There were no tall buildings to conceal its resplendent beauty, only miles and miles of rolling farmland to bathe in its soft rosy radiance. With great pain, she recalled the last sunset she had watched with Luke.

They had stepped out of the barn just as the daily spectacle was taking place. They had paused to watch the fiery round ball slide gently behind a hilltop and disappear. The sky was still ablaze with reds and oranges and they had both looked at each other and smiled. They had shared a beautiful moment together. . . .

A soft knock sounded on her door and she turned away from the window, hurriedly dabbing at her eyes.

"Yes?"

Ed Flannery stuck his head in the door and smiled. "I'll spring for the pizza if you'll buy the suds."

She shook her head and smiled back. "Thanks, Ed, but I'm going to be here at least another two or three hours."

"Again?" Ed was an attractive man whom she had dated several times in the past and he was always fun to be with. In a way she was tempted to accept his offer. It would be good to laugh again. But she would make miserable company and she knew it.

"Yes, I'm afraid so. I can't seem to get caught up."

"Well, I'm pretty good at lending a helping hand," he offered lightly.

"That's really nice of you, Ed, but most of it is a one-man job. Thanks anyway for the offer."

"Sure thing. Don't work too late," he cautioned.

"No, I won't."

But it was past eleven when she finally let herself into her apartment and switched on the light. She glanced at her watch again. It was late, but Texas was in a different time zone. . . .

Her mind toyed with calling Luke just to say hello and see if he thought Uriah was doing as well as had been reported. It was a viable excuse, even if it was sort of a lame one. Before she lost her nerve she jerked up the receiver and hurriedly punched out his number by memory.

The phone rang for a very long time before he finally answered. "Dr. Travers here."

Her knees turned weak at the sound of his voice and she was afraid she was going to lose her nerve and hang up.

"Dr. Travers!" he barked again.

Would he think she was out of line by calling him this way? Probably. And what if he was with Marilyn or entertaining some other woman from Rueter Flats? She suddenly felt sick to her stomach as she hurriedly placed the phone back in its cradle.

For the next few minutes she paced the floor in front of the phone, reviewing all the reasons why he should be the one to call her. But when all the evidence had been presented she decided he really didn't have more of a reason to call her than she did him.

The fact was, she had more. She wanted to know about Uriah.

Quickly snatching up the phone once more, she

punched out the numbers and waited while it rang only twice this time.

"Dr. Travers."

And once again she was struck speechless and hung up.

But the third time his phone rang the receiver was snatched up on the first summons and an impatient voice boomed out, "Damnit, Cassie! If you're going to keep getting me out of the shower the least you can do is say something!"

For a moment she was so astounded that he would know who was calling, she couldn't talk.

"Cass," he admonished sharply.

"What?" Her thoughts were now honed in on the fact that she had gotten him out of the shower. He must be standing there dripping wet . . . nude . . . nude . . . nude. . . .

He let out a rush of relieved breath. "Then it is you," he confirmed softly.

"Yes. How in the world did you know?"

Maybe it was because he had spent the last three weeks thinking about her every hour of the day. Maybe because every time the phone rang he had been praying it would be her. Maybe he had suddenly turned psychic. He couldn't explain it. Somehow, he just knew.

"I don't know . . . I just did." He propped a wet hip on the side of the cabinet and closed his eyes for a moment, visualizing the curve of her mouth, the way it was moist and sweet when he kissed her. "What's up, babe?" What's up, babe! Couldn't he think of anything more eloquent to say to her than "What's up, babe?" he agonized. Couldn't he tell her how much he had missed her, how he was dying inside day by day, how he longed to touch her, to taste her. . . .

"Nothing." She closed her eyes and tried to remember his touch . . . his smell. The musky aroma that sent her blood pounding through her chest and her senses reeling. . . . "I was just wondering how everything was going back there."

"About the same."

"Have you seen Dad lately?"

"Yeah, Wylie and I took in a movie last night. I visited with Uriah awhile when we got back."

"Is he doing as well as Mom says he is?"

"Seems to be. His color's back to normal and his appetite's picking up."

"Oh, good. Good." Say you miss me, you big oaf! Tell me since I've gone your life's been as miserable and bleak as mine has!

"How's the Big Apple?"

"Hot."

Ha. She didn't know the meaning of the word. He bet it couldn't hold a candle to the way he had been since she had left. "Yeah. It's been warm here too."

She bit her lower lip thoughtfully. "You ever been to New York?"

"No, never have."

"No? Oh, that's terrible. Everyone should see New York at least once in their lifetime."

"Yeah, that's what they say." Just say the word, babe, and I'll be up there so quick it'll make your head swim, he pleaded silently.

All right, you stubborn jackass! I'm going to make a complete fool out of myself and ask, but I'm warning you—you better not laugh in my face!

177

"Why don't you fly up here sometime? I'd be glad to show you the sights," she offered nonchalantly, then held her breath as she waited for his answer.

"Fly up there?" He managed to sound as if the idea had never occurred to him. He reached over on the counter and fumbled for a smoke with trembling hands. "Uh . . . when would be a good time for you?"

Good time? Good time? She willed herself to think straight. It was already late Thursday night. Should she dare invite him for this weekend?

His alleged state of undress on the other end thundered through her mind like a herd of wild buffalo. The width of his chest, the touch of his hand, the way the tight muscles in his forearms gathered tautly when he held her in his arms. . . . "Would this weekend be convenient?" she inquired meekly.

"This weekend?" His insides jumped with anticipation. "Sure, that sounds all right to me." He reached over and draped a towel around his middle as the tension in his loins steadily increased.

"You can? Great!" She clapped her hand over her mouth and was mortified that she had been so appallingly transparent.

Grinning to himself, he fought to remind himself this was not to be taken as a sign that she actually cared and had missed him. She was probably experiencing just a touch of homesickness. "Why not? I think I can get Milt Turner to take my calls for the weekend."

Clearing her throat nervously, she managed to regain a thread of her composure. "Oh, well that will be wonderful. I'll pick you up at the airport."

Since he would be flying his private plane, they discussed his possible arrival time the following evening and she assured him she would be there waiting for him.

"Great! I'll see you tomorrow afternoon."

"Well . . . good night. . . . Oh, I hope I didn't call too late."

"No. I hadn't gone to bed yet."

Was he alone? God, let him be alone. "Uh, you don't have company, do you?"

"No. Why?"

"Oh, I just thought I heard voices in the background."

"The television is on, that's probably what you hear."

Once more a tremendous sense of relief washed over her. "Yes . . . well . . . good night again." "My darling" she added silently.

"Yeah . . . good night." "My love" he added silently.

Then they both hung up to spend another restless night alone.

When the blue and white, twin-engine Cessna came rolling into the hangar late Friday afternoon, Cassie was there, jumping up and down, waving exuberantly at the pilot.

There was something to be said for discretion, but she couldn't think of it at the moment.

Luke climbed out of the cockpit as she ran across the tarmac to meet him.

Did she throw herself in his arms and kiss him

179

senseless, like she longed to do, or did she wait to see how he would greet her?

Deciding that it would be prudent to rely on the latter, her steps slowed and she waited until he gathered his belongings and began to walk toward her.

Her eyes eagerly drank in the familiar sight and her smile was nothing less than radiant as he approached carrying a blue garment bag draped casually over his shoulder and held by the tips of two fingers.

He paused when he reached her and they looked at each other hungrily.

You're even more beautiful than I remembered, his eyes told her wordlessly.

How could I ever have thought I could live without you, her gaze confessed lovingly.

"How was the flight?"

"Not bad. A little bumpy at times." He glanced around him. "Big place."

She laughed. "Yes, pretty good size."

They fell into step with one another and started in the direction of her car. They talked about the weather and Uriah. He told her Wylie's baseball team had won the championship last week and Rosalee was wearing maternity clothes again.

When they reached the car he paused and looked at the plain two-door sedan parked at the curb. "Where's the Jag?"

"In the body shop. This is a loaner."

"Did you wreck your car?"

"No, just having the hurricane 'Rueter Flats' corrected." She grinned.

On the way home she made several detours to point out various sights she thought he should see and he

180

was clearly impressed by the city. They decided it was still too early for dinner, at least by New York standards, so she drove directly to her apartment to rest for a while before they began the tour of the city she had so lavishly planned.

When they arrived she took him on a brief excursion of the two-bedroom flat and almost popped a button when he told her it was nice. Really nice. And she wanted to hug his neck when she realized he was sincere.

Gliding over to the window, she pushed a button and the drapes gracefully folded away, revealing a spectacular view below them. The lights of the city were just beginning to twinkle on—a beautiful, breathtaking sight—and Luke chuckled and said he felt like he was in a spaceship looking out.

They stood gazing over the vista, saying nothing for a moment. It just felt good to stand there next to each other and know they were together again.

Her hand hesitantly slid over and reached for his.

His hand closed over hers warmly.

They turned and their eyes met in the gathering twilight.

"Hello," she said softly.

"Hello," he said in the same tone.

She wasn't sure how she suddenly found herself in his arms, or how they were suddenly kissing with a wild, insatiable urgency, or how he was murmuring her name over and over in a husky, pleading voice as he lifted her into his arms and carried her into the bedroom—but it all happened. The only thing she was totally sure of was the love they shared in that next glorious two hours.

Somehow the unbelievable ecstasy they found in each other's arms seemed to make up for all the loneliness and agony of the past few weeks.

Darkness had long ago spread its velvet mantle across the city when their frenzied lovemaking slowed then finally abated.

They were still lying in the ebony shadows, leisurely exchanging long, drugging kisses when the mantel clock struck ten. The searing urgency was over now. They could simply lie in each other's arms, contented, happy . . . at peace with themselves and the world for the first time in a long time.

"Are you getting hungry?" she asked sleepily.

"I think I could eat a ten-pound steak," he acknowledged in the same drowsy voice. He was sprawled flat on his stomach, dozing now.

She slid on top of his back and hugged him tightly. "I know where they have delicious steaks and huge baked potatoes dripping with butter and sour cream and chives. . . ."

He grunted as her weight smashed his nose farther down in his pillow. "If you'll quit trying to smother me, I'll let you take me there," he promised in a muffled voice.

"I will grant you your life on only one condition," she threatened.

"What's the condition?" His voice was even more drowned out as she suddenly sat up and smacked his bare bottom affectionately.

"I want you to say it."

"Say what?"

This was his hour of reckoning. She had come to grips with hers long ago.

Not once had he told her he loved her, but she knew he did. She just knew it. And he wasn't going to leave this bed until she heard him admit it!

For agonizingly long moments he didn't say anything and she felt like she suddenly had a hedge apple wedged in her throat. What was he waiting for? Would he actually pretend indifference and say "You didn't really take all of this seriously, did you?"

But he didn't. Instead, he slowly removed the pillow off his head and rolled over. It was dark in the room, so she couldn't see his face, but she knew by the timbre of his voice, he was stunned by her request. "You want me to say I'm in love with you?"

Her eyes dropped shyly, then she laid her head on his chest so she wouldn't have to look at him. "Yes . . . Oh, Luke, I think I'm going to die if I don't hear you say those words."

He suddenly felt as if all the air had gone out of him. "You wouldn't . . . laugh at me if I did?"

Her head snapped up. "Laugh at you!"

"Yes! Laugh at me." He reached out and cupped her face between his two large hands and his gaze bore into hers solemnly. "You think I haven't wanted to tell you that I love you—you think I haven't died a thousand deaths knowing that I've fallen in love with a woman who couldn't stand the sight of me. . . ."

"Oh, that was years ago," she scoffed. "I was young and foolish—"

"And a mean, feisty little heifer," he added tartly, "that wouldn't have thought twice about slicing my heart out and feeding it to her dad's hogs."

She blushed at his callous—yet surprisingly astute—

assessment of her earlier feelings. "Now, really, Luke, I wasn't that bad, was I?"

"Every bit and more."

"Well, you weren't exactly Mr. Nice Guy yourself. I remember all the bad times you gave me," she defended.

He waved off her objections curtly. "I was only fighting fire with fire."

"Well, I'm tired of fighting," she announced.

"Oh?" His left brow came up challengingly. "Well, what do you want me to do about it?"

She grinned and he blushed. "Say that no matter how cantankerous I was, you managed to fall in love with me anyway."

With a gentle touch of his hand to her cheek, he complied willingly. "That's too easy. I do love you, you feisty little heifer."

"Say it nicely!"

He flashed her a contrite grin. "I love you, darling. I think I always have."

And then they were back in each other's arms once more, pouring out their love, their words tumbling over each other's in their eagerness to confess what they had felt all along. The hours slipped away and dinner was completely forgotten.

The following day proved to be hectic. Cassie had planned enough activities for an entire week, so they were kept busy from early morning until late evening. When they had seen all they could see by daylight, Luke took her up in the plane and they flew over New York at night.

But even though they had finally confessed their

love, they still couldn't bring themselves to discuss the future.

For Luke the future still loomed bleakly ahead, since he knew her feelings concerning Rueter Flats and he had no idea what he could do to change them.

For Cassie the decision had not been easy, although a relatively simple one. She knew what she was going to do about it.

So when Sunday afternoon was upon them and it was time for Luke to leave and he still hadn't said anything about their future, she resigned herself to the fact that she would have to make the first move again.

But that didn't bother her. She loved him enough, and even more, to do that. Still, she wanted to see if he would actually depart without proposing to her.

They had arrived at the airport a little before two, and she had walked to the plane with him. He had been pensive all day, a little jumpy, a little irritable, yet so darn lovable they had made love twice before they left the apartment.

"Be careful," she warned as he slid his gear into the plane. "I'm not sure I like these small planes." Actually she wasn't sure she liked any plane. They all made her want to throw up.

"I'm always careful." He draped the garment bag over the passenger seat and turned around to kiss her again.

They stood locked in a passionate embrace, kissing and patting and hugging until she was sure the men in the control tower wished they'd get on with it.

"I can't tell you how nice it's been to have you," she teased in a pleasant voice. "You have to promise to look me up if you ever get up this way again."

185

He eyed her sourly. "I'll do that. And you be sure and do the same when you're in Rueter Flats."

She nodded solemnly. "Oh, I will."

"Well." He cast a hesitant glance around him. How in the hell was he going to leave her here? What would she say if he got down on his knees and begged her to go home with him? No—she wouldn't go. She still had her fancy job and hated small-town living. "Guess I should be shovin' off."

That's right, you stubborn, adorable oaf! Just stand there and ignore the fact we just spent a weekend that will change our lives forever. "Yeah, I guess it's a pretty long flight."

"Yeah . . . pretty long."

He gazed at her longingly. "Cass . . ."

"Yes?" She smiled at him, trying to give him the courage he was so desperately seeking.

But once again his shoulders sagged dejectedly and he let out a long sigh. "Nothing. I'll give you a call sometime next week."

"Okay."

He kissed her once more and then turned to climb aboard the plane.

"Luke."

He turned. "Yes?"

"Aren't you even going to help a lady with her luggage?"

"Her luggage?" he asked blankly.

"Yes. There're four bags in the trunk of the car, and then we have to take the car to the parking area because the body shop is coming over to pick it up tomorrow morning, then I'll have to fly back soon to pick up the Jag and take care of the lease—"

"Hold it!" Luke slid off the plane slowly. "What are you yammering about?"

"Yammering? Really, Luke. Yammering? I'm standing here about to ask you to marry me and you accuse me of yammering?" She shook her head chidingly.

His face was totally confused by now. He shifted his weight to one foot and put his hand on his hip. "You're asking *me* to marry you?"

"Yes! You will—won't you?" Suddenly all her earlier bravado started to falter. What if he wouldn't? She couldn't stand it, that's what!

Keeping his face without expression, he reached into his pocket and withdrew a cigar. Inside he felt like jumping for joy, but he couldn't believe this was for real just yet. "What about your job?"

"Oh, haven't you heard? I've decided to open up my own advertising agency in Macon." She was still holding her breath, hoping. . . .

"And that fancy promotion?"

"Being my own boss is better."

He struck a match and lit the smoke. Then, holding the cigar in his even white teeth, his eyes narrowed in challenge as he said, "Oh, yeah? Well what about living in Rueter Flats again?"

She shrugged sheepishly. "Mom and Dad are getting older. I need to be around more often . . . and my nieces and nephews need to get to know their Aunt Cassie a little better."

"Well," he took a long, thoughtful drag off the cigar, pretending to think about her proposal. When he saw the absolutely miserable look keep deepening on her face, he quickly discarded his insincere theatrics.

"Well, hell. Why not?" He grinned and winked at her conspiratorially. "The town could use a little class."

She returned his grin, ear to ear, replying in her worst Rueter Flats drawl, "Ain't that the ever-lovin' truth, sugggaarrr!"

Then their faces grew serious, and they held each other for a long, loving moment.

They quickly disposed of the car and gathered up her luggage, pausing to clasp each other in lingering smoldering kisses every now and then.

Within thirty minutes they were walking back across the tarmac and Cassie was yammering away happily.

"Now, I want to make one thing perfectly clear. Just because I gave in first doesn't mean I'm going to be a real pushover after we're married," she was saying as he proceeded to help her into the plane. "I still plan on having my career and my life—"

"I sort of had that one figured out all by myself," Luke said dryly.

"And there are still things I will never change my opinion on. Number one! You are not going to keep me barefoot and pregnant all the time. . , ."

He pinched her on her behind affectionately. "I have every intention of keeping you in shoes!"

She turned around and shot him a dour look. "Having shoes is not what I was worried about." She proceeded to climb into the plane. "Now, maybe someday we'll have one—possibly two children, but I certainly don't plan on being like the other women of Rueter Flats who have a baby every nine months like clockwork—and I seriously doubt if you will ever catch me in Nellie Sooter's beauty shop having one of her revolting permanents. In fact, you may even have to fly me back up here occasionally so I can go shopping and let Stephan do my hair—and do you realize, Luke Travers, I don't even know your middle name—"

"Luke Raymond," he supplied easily.

She whirled around and her mouth dropped open weakly. "Your middle name is . . . Raymond?"

He nodded. "Yeah, why?"

"Oh, no reason." She sank down on her seat lamely, realizing what they would probably name their first son.

But there would be only one Ray among her children—no more!

"What's yours?"

"Cassandra Beth."

Leaning over to fasten her seat belt, his mouth found hers again in the process. "Hello, Cassandra Beth."

She sighed hopelessly. "Hello, my darling, Luke Raymond."

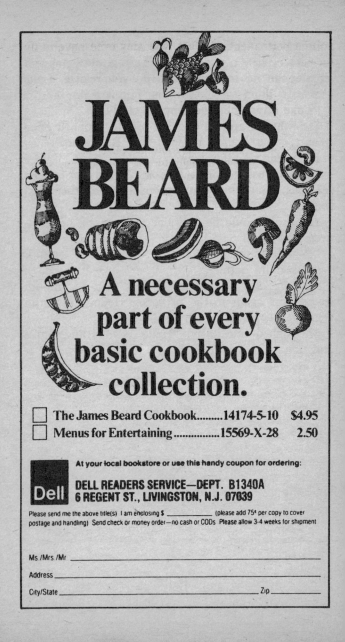

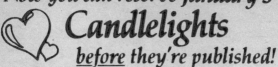
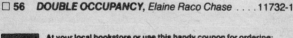